between camelots

Drue Heinz Literature Prize 2005

between
Camelots

DAVID HARRIS EBENBACH

University of Pittsburgh Press

Published by the University of Pittsburgh Press, Pittsburgh, PA 15260

Manufactured in the United States of America
Printed on acid-free paper
10 9 8 7 6 5 4 3 2 1

Library of Congress Cataloging-in-Publication Data
Ebenbach, David Harris.
  Between Camelots / David Harris Ebenbach.
    p. cm.
  "Drue Heinz Literature Prize 2005."
  ISBN 0-8229-4268-2 (acid-free paper)
  1. United States—Social life and customs—Fiction. 2. Psychological
fiction, American. 3. Loss (Psychology)—Fiction. I. Title.
  PS3605.B46B48 2005
  813'.6—dc22
                                        2005014145

For Rachel,

by whose light

all the world's possibilities

are visible.

Contents

between camelots

Misdirections

MY WIFE is using the mice as an excuse to let our marriage
fall apart. All night they crawl around in our walls and we can
hear them gnawing. They're gnawing at the foundation of our
marriage, she says. She complains I won't do anything about them,
or about anything else, and that's the problem. Neither of us men-
tions the man whose sweat she smells like these days.

But I put out humane traps, little plastic opaque boxes for
them to get cornered in. Our son loads the peanut butter into
the back ends. That same evening, we've got our first mouse. The
box rattles on the kitchen tiles.

My son and I are going to go release it by the lake, and he
asks his mother to come. He knows and doesn't know. She wipes
her hands dry and reluctantly agrees.

I can feel the mouse moving in the box as we walk down
Jenifer Street. Because it's a strange feeling, I let my son carry it
a while. He squeals with the thrill of it, but my wife is silent.

I think of something. I ask my son, "What if it finds its way
back?" His eyes grow wide.

"It's three blocks," my wife says. "The mouse isn't that smart."

"Well, maybe," I say loudly, and wink at my son. "I just hope it doesn't remember to head for *Spaight Street*, and *turn left*, and go to the *fifth house*." That's not how you get to our house. I'm giving the mouse misdirections. My son laughs, excited. Despite herself, so does my wife.

She looks at me and then at our son. Surprising me, she says, "I hope the thing doesn't tell all the other mice about our house on *Spaight*, either."

Soon we're all giving loud misdirections, just like a family.

By the lake, we all stoop down and I prepare to let the mouse go. Our son has his eyes wide and mouth open, surprised and awed in advance. I look up at my wife and she is looking at me, expectant, hopeful. This mouse, I think, is giving me my family back. Lowering the box to the ground, I put my finger on the little door, ready. I am almost asking her, with my eyes, whether we might keep the mouse. *Can we?* When she sees that question, though, her face answers by sinking out of its smile. She sighs and looks away from me.

I open the door. Before I've even caught sight of the mouse, it's completely gone.

Rue Rachel

WHEN SHE woke up on the train, lying across two seats under her mink coat, her turquoise sneakers poking out into the aisle, Rachel didn't know where she was for a minute. Dizzy from the sleep and the pills, she lifted up on an elbow and looked out the window at fields of snow. "My *god*," she said. She was supposed to be in a class, psychology or econ, depending on what time it was, but instead she was on her way to Montreal. Rachel let her head fall back down, her long, dark hair spreading around her.

The only reason she was going to see Adrien was because she was worried about him and what was happening to him up there. It wasn't like she was *with* him, though she had mentioned him significantly to that guy on the train who had helped her with her bag, just so there was no mistake about her being interested in anything.

"My boyfriend should be here helping me," she had said, popping her gum at her helper. "But he's in Montreal, at McGill. That's why I'm going."

The man lifting her bag, redheaded and scruffy and with paint on his clothes, said, "Great," like he meant that it was really great.

"Yeah," she said. "He needs me." She knew Adrien was hanging out with guys who were heavy into clubbing and other things. Even after a month, when he came back down to visit, he was all skinny and distracted.

Rachel hated the train. She went back to sleep and slept as much as she could, and in between naps she woke up with itchy skin and a sense of everything happening slowly. She knew about side effects. Her father was a doctor. Twice she found the scruffy redheaded man, who was reading some book, and she sat down across the aisle and told him things about herself.

"I'm from Manhasset," she said. "On Long Island. I don't know any French." And she stared at the light brown bowls of his eyes and saw patterns in his facial hair, and she scratched her thighs. The man seemed like he didn't have much to say.

When the customs woman came through the car, Rachel said she had nothing to declare, even though actually she was bringing three cartons of Camel Lights to Adrien. You couldn't get them in Montreal. The woman asked her basically the same question again and again. "You didn't bring any gifts?" she said. "You're visiting someone without gifts?" Rachel hated her. The woman was like Adrien's mother, who she also hated. Like she owned the world.

Then, after all the blank whiteness of upstate New York, the lights of Montreal finally made their little show outside the window.

Adrien met her at the station. It was not like Penn Station; it was too empty. Adrien, skinny and tall, stood in the middle of it like a stop sign. She handed him her suitcase to roll.

"I can't believe I came here," she said. "Where am I?" He had been trying to hug her when she started talking. Now he said, "Okay. Let's go." She could hear the accent. He was born in France, and sometimes she could hear it. Rachel had been to France. It was no big thing to go there.

As they walked to the doors to get to the taxis in all the snow, she saw the redheaded man walking toward the Metro sign. Everyone talked about the Metro in Montreal. She didn't understand what was supposed to be so great about it.

Instead of going back to his apartment first, to drop off the suitcase, Adrien took her straight to this restaurant that served crepes, on a street called Rue Rachel. When the taxi dropped them off at the snow-clogged intersection, Adrien pointed up at the sign. *Rue Rachel.* "See that?" he said.

She did see that. It was kind of nice. Unexpected. "Is it a long street?" she said.

He nodded. "It runs all the way northeast—" he pointed— "from the Parc Mont-Royal." She was staring at him. She still felt sleepy from the pills and the train. "It's very long," he said.

"That's nice," she said, and she leaned against him, her fur coat on his wool one. Then she straightened up. "My back hurts. We should go to the restaurant and you can rub my back."

Inside, she squirmed against her seat while he ordered for them in French. The language sounded deceptive to her. Then he noticed her squirming and he reached out to squeeze the muscle in her shoulder. Just then, though, she didn't want him to do that. His dark curly hair had been made funny by his winter hat, and it needed to be cut. Also, the restaurant was full of old people eating themselves to death.

"Are we going to a club tonight?" she said.

5

"Sure," he said.

"Thank god." She bent her arm to pinch that same muscle in her shoulder. Her other hand dropped the fork. "I have the drops," she said. A lot of times she got that way during classes, when the pills would make it hard to hold on to her pencils or pens, and her friends would tease her. They were pretty fun friends, except maybe Jen. It'd be nice to have them around tonight. "What?" she said. Adrien had said something that she'd missed.

"I asked if you were on those pills again."

Rachel looked at him with her chin in her hand. She wished they could have gone back to his place first so she could have changed clothes, but maybe it was better this way. Once, she was at his apartment in New York, and she was in the shower, pretty sleepy from stuff, and she fell and landed on her back on the edge of the bathtub. And Adrien had run in, but when he saw her, he just started laughing. Then he took her to bed so she could rest and in a few minutes they were having sex, with her hair still wet and her back hurting.

"You haven't said anything sweet to me yet," she said now in the restaurant. "I was on the train all day to come here."

"I didn't?" he said, reaching across for her hand. She let him hold it. He started to say something, but she interrupted.

"I mean, do you love me? Not like that, I mean, but do you?"

He pulled his hand off and opened his mouth.

"Don't talk to me about pills," she said in a flash of anger. "At least I don't take crystal meth."

He looked around, nervous. "Jesus," he said.

She rolled her eyes. It wasn't like she had said it in French.

They went back to his apartment to change clothes. It was cold, but bigger than the apartment he used to have in Manhattan. That was something.

"Well, so what *do* you want to do tonight?" Adrien said at one point while she was getting ready, his long arms up in the air. Rachel had just been saying some things about not wanting to hang out with his friends, and before that had just pushed Adrien's hands off her tits. She had been sitting in front of the mirror and he came up from behind and put his hands on her tits. Then they were both in the mirror, him with his arms in the air, and her holding a hairbrush.

Then they met up with a couple of Adrien's friends, both of them Quebecois, both excited about the Camel Lights. Everybody was in these winter coats and hats, and you couldn't see what anybody really looked like. But right away she got the idea that she didn't like Martin, whose name was pronounced Mar*tan*, and who seemed like he was all superior and condescending or something. He definitely had an accent. The other guy, Patrick, she couldn't tell.

Now they walked together down some sidewalk covered in unshoveled snow toward a club that played hip-hop. She had her fur coat on, but she was still cold.

"Maybe you should eat more," Martin said when she complained. "Grow bigger and warmer." Adrien was walking with Patrick, the two of them smoking.

She sneered at him. *Fuck you,* she thought. *At least I'm not on crystal meth.*

The club was crowded and the music was thundering. Adrien shouted that it was supposed to be the biggest dance floor in

Canada, and pulled her onto it right away. It was definitely big. Rachel felt unsteady but settled into some easy movements with her hips while Adrien bumped up into her, and when he did, she could feel his dick in his pants. Every time she moved she was going between that and all the other bodies. All these people in Montreal, she could tell, were really impressed with themselves. After a while she went and sat down and Adrien followed her to the table. Patrick had ordered everybody mojitos and the glasses were already sitting on the table.

"I'm sorry," she said, loud, over the bass. "I can't drink that."

"What?" Patrick said.

Adrien rolled his eyes. "She has to watch her drink every minute now."

Rachel looked at him and hated him. She would never marry a guy who would be like that. She turned to Patrick and said, shouting, "I have this crazy girlfriend who carries around a Snapple bottle of GHB."

"Of what?" Patrick said. He wore glasses, in a good-looking way.

Adrien laughed. "Date-rape drug," he said.

Patrick seemed stunned. "She carries a bottle of date-rape drug?"

"I know," Rachel said. "My god. She takes it herself. She likes the way it feels." Martin showed up now and sat down.

Patrick's eyes and mouth were wide open. "She gives *herself* the date-rape drug?"

"*And* me, one time," Rachel said. She remembered that feeling, slipping away, slipping down and away. "She secretly put some in my drink so I'd be like on her level. She does that all the time to people. She's crazy. So now I have to watch to make sure nobody does that to me again."

"But what happened next with your girlfriend?" Martin said, smiling and licking his lips in a dirty way.

Rachel gave him another sneer. "We did it *all night*," she said, making sure the sarcasm was really obvious.

Martin stood up. "Well, I have to go jerk off in the bathroom now," he said, smiling lopsided. And he looked at Adrien, said, "You want to come?" Rachel glared at everybody. Martin was secretly talking about going to get some drugs.

Adrien looked at her, and she said, "Whatever," not really loud enough to be heard over the music, and looked around for a waitress so she could get her own drink. She remembered she was here to save Adrien, but couldn't make herself deal with that now. He shrugged and got up and went off with Martin.

Rachel herself drew the line between prescription drugs and illegal ones. She looked over at Patrick, who was staring at her. The music was really deafening.

"Why would anybody move to Montreal?" she said, even louder than she needed to be. "My god."

Patrick blinked, surprised. "I was born in Quebec," he said.

"Oh," she said. "I'm sorry." She paused a minute. "So tell me what's so great about it."

He frowned like he was really thinking hard. "I like all of it," he said, watching her face, trying to come up with a good answer. She could tell he was a decent kind of guy. "Okay," he said. "I lave you been to Parc la Fontaine?"

She shook her head.

"Well, it's got a very shallow lake in it," he said. He really didn't have a big accent. "And it freezes in the winter, and the families all come there to skate, and the college students, and you have couples holding hands and skating, and . . . I mean, there are these frozen ponds all over Canada, but, I don't know, it's different somehow in this one place. It's like that Brueghel painting. You know?" He was talking fast. "And I remember these two little children in big puffy jackets once just falling all over the ice like little pillows, orange and blue, and all around them these students and businessmen skating, and soon they'll all go off to a café and talk, and—"

The waitress came then and got a drink order from Rachel, and she seemed really happy to be a waitress. Rachel turned back and saw Patrick looking kind of like afraid of something.

"Wow," she said. "Huh." She didn't know what he was talking about.

"I'm not explaining what I mean," Patrick said.

"It's okay," Rachel said, picking up her mojito glass and putting it down again.

After a few hours, they all ended up walking around outside, even though it was freezing, because Adrien and Martin were full of energy.

"I want you to see the city," Adrien said to her.

"I'm cold."

"C'mon. You're going to see how great it is."

They walked up St. Laurent and over to Rue Rachel again, with Adrien really making a big show about that, and down St. Denis, and across Ste. Catherine, and Rachel's feet got colder and colder. It was hard to walk on the snow in her shoes, and mostly she looked down to make sure she didn't fall. Adrien and Martin told her to look at all the ethnic restaurants, all the bars, all the clubs, the shops, the people walking the same sidewalks despite the temperature, which was even more ridiculous than before. Patrick, who was mostly quiet now and who split off from them before long, had pointed out the stairs that wound up from the street to the houses' front doors. Rachel didn't understand any of it. She wanted to ask where the mountain was. There was supposed to be a mountain here. But it couldn't be that tall anyway, if she couldn't already see it.

It was late when they got back to Adrien's place. He kissed her when they were inside, and he smelled like the alcohol and the smoke and everything else he'd done.

When they were in bed, Rachel just moved down the bed and pulled down his pants and underpants to put his dick in her mouth, because it was the easiest thing. But first she held it in her hand and then she squeezed it once, hard.

"Jesus! Rach!" he said.

Then she put his dick in her mouth. This part was easy.

When she was a little girl, Rachel had gone ice-skating a lot. She could skate backwards and spin, and liked the way she imagined she looked in a pink coat, spinning. She made a picture of that in her head when Adrien finally fell asleep, and held onto it for a while. In her mind, she turned and turned in that pink coat, and she could see herself from all sides.

She looked over at Adrien's face. His eyes were closed and his mouth was open. She hated him. She was going to get on a train early in the morning and leave him here with all his problems and his friends. It didn't matter to her whether he was in trouble or not. She could never marry a man like that.

Even in the bed Rachel was cold. She wondered where her clothes were. And then she wondered what Montreal was like in the summer, if it was better when there wasn't so much snow and cold. And then she thought of Patrick's pond melting and nobody able to skate on it. Something about that made her want to cry. Earlier that night Adrien had said that Rue Rachel ran right up alongside a park—maybe it was the one Patrick had been talking about. She started to cry, not sure whether to wish for warm weather or not. All she knew was that somewhere in this city was a man who, no matter what, would just be looking forward to winter again.

Between Camelots

WHEN PAUL got to the house, the first thing he did was stand in the driveway to listen to the sounds of the barbecue going on in the backyard. He heard a large number of voices coming from there, more than a couple of conversations, all concentrated off in the near distance, all out of sight. He had passed other such focal points of sound along the way; there were probably many barbecues tonight. He stood still and listened in.

Then Marianna appeared from the back carrying a garbage bag to leave by the garage, and as soon as she saw Paul there, she was already talking, and talking about what he was thinking about. "Wow—hi! You're here! Did you walk the whole way? Well. Julie's not here yet," she said, her long blond hair bobbing like party streamers around her grinning, freckled face, "but I'm pretty sure she's coming. Did you bring veggie burgers? We don't have any. But we've got beer—I'll show you around back." They went around back.

Paul and Marianna both worked downtown at the Governor's Institute for Health Research. She was in public relations, and he was in statistical analysis. He was there to do things like explore the relationships between life crises, personality traits, poverty, and sick days. They had very different lives, he supposed. Sometimes she stood at the door to his office, between meetings, and told him about the people she'd met over the weekend. They were daunting in their quantity and in their diversity. A married Brazilian couple getting twin doctorates in communicative disorders, a young rabbi with raffle tickets, a little girl with an enormous vocabulary and a broken nose, the firemen sitting around on Palance Street. Paul heard these stories and wanted to love Marianna.

Out back, her husband Ben greeted him warmly. He held a bock beer as though his hand had always been meant to hold a beer, and he clapped Paul on the shoulder. "Good to see you again," he said. His arm swept wide to indicate the small backyard, the people already clustered comfortably within it. "Welcome to the estate."

"It smells like the grill's almost ready," Paul said. Ben told him it would be a while.

Paul took his veggie burgers inside to the freezer and found the beer. Nothing had changed since seventh-grade school dances, he realized—he had to keep his hands busy with refreshments so as not to feel like an idiot.

Their kitchen, a little thing split into pieces by aggressive counters, smelled like dried herbs and spices. He saw all the things they had that only married people have—a four-slot toaster, a waffle iron, glasses that matched plates. In the refrigerator he noticed a whole head of lettuce, too enormous for any one person alone.

Through the door, he again heard the voices of people he didn't know. Familiar people sound unique, distinct, he thought, because you hear them with more parts of you. Unfamiliar people, though, make noises like foreign languages.

He stepped outside again, expecting Ben to congratulate him on finding the beer, but he and Marianna were holding court by the grill, telling another couple about the tentless camping vacation they'd just taken. Paul looked around for an open conversation. Then he moved toward the food instead. He dug deeply into the jalapeño cheese dip with blue corn chips. Meanwhile, he concentrated until his facial muscles, he hoped, gave off the impression that he was casual and approachable.

Lately he'd been afraid of these kinds of gatherings, but here he was. He was mostly here because of this Julie, a woman Marianna had just met at a wedding in town. The Monday after, Marianna, the only one of Paul's acquaintances who still found something remarkable in his loneliness, described Julie to him from his office door. "She's striking," she said, "absolutely striking. I mean, she's enormously tall. Imposing, you know? She's an imposing presence."

Paul frowned. "She sounds scary," he said.

"No, no. I said she's striking—Julie has a really interesting face."

Paul imagined her lumbering into Marianna's backyard, sweeping aside with leglike arms the high tree branches that blocked her path. But it would have to, at the very least, he hoped, provide a story for his journal later on, when he started his nightly routine over again. Masturbation, sighing journal entries, and then to bed—a bed that had gone unshared so long that he'd developed an elaborate system of arranging his four pillows for maximum comfort, outside of which he could hardly fall asleep.

A young man with a shaved head now walked up to the table with his eyes locked intensely on the chips. As a side gesture, he introduced himself to Paul, extending his right hand across his white Speed Racer T-shirt to be shaken. "Max," he said, articulating the name exaggeratedly, showing a flash of teeth.

Paul introduced himself, looked down at the browning grass, and then, with a conscious effort, asked Max whether he was a friend of Marianna's.

"No. I just snuck in off the street," he smirked.

Paul didn't know what to say. "That dip is homemade, I think," he offered.

Max looked over and ran a hand over his stubbled scalp, pursing his lips. "That's not always a good thing." He seemed hesitant to continue, but then he did, absently. "So. What's your story? Who do you know here?"

"Marianna," Paul said. She was still by the grill, and the rest of the guests, all young professional types with glasses, moved around the little backyard as though affected by her gravity— even people walking at a distance from her took curving paths to acknowledge their hostess. She occasionally poked the coals with a stick, and Ben rubbed the small of her back. Paul wished she'd catch his eye and draw him in.

"It's an interesting crowd of folks," Max said. "You should meet them."

"Oh, yeah?"

"Well, actually in fact I don't have any opinion about them at all. I'm just talking. Maybe you like these kinds of people—I don't keep a lot of friends, myself," he continued.

"What? You don't?" Paul asked, sneaking a chip from the bowl in front of Max.

"I gave up on it. One too many Camelots."

"Camelots?" Paul said, burrowing into the cheese dip again. A couple of new people appeared in the backyard, but none of them looked like they could be this Julie.

"Oh, yes," Max said, thoughtful. "My teen years and my early twenties were all about going from Camelot to Camelot. These large groups of friends get together, and everybody loves everybody, and then somebody sleeps with the wrong somebody or everybody moves somewhere else, and the whole thing collapses again. Up and down, up and down, up and down. Who can put up with that? Do you know what I mean?"

"Why's it so bad?"

"It's unstable," Max said, punctuating his point with his finger in the air. "More instability in an unnecessarily chaotic world I'm for stability."

Paul tried to decide if he agreed with this conceptualization of things, thinking about his own life. He'd had a circle of friends in high school that did everything together, including a lot of drinking on rocky beaches, which almost killed him one night. He had lost track of them through college. Then he'd had a utopian relationship with a botany major his senior year, until she realized how wrong it had all been from the start. And it's true—he'd slept with the wrong people in graduate school, starting up the newest phase of desertification in his social life. "But maybe you didn't really break the cycle after all," he said. "How do you know you're not just *between* Camelots now?"

Max looked at him as though astounded. "Because of a particular thing called *free will*," he said. "I have *chosen* to be *done* with that kind of life. For example, I'll tell you what—here we are, getting along, but at the end of this conversation, I'm not going to give you my phone number or my e-mail address, or anything, and I won't take anything from you. Simple."

"Huh," Paul said.

"So—as advertised, I'm going to take off," Max said, grabbing an enormous handful of chips. He winked and wandered off toward another group of people, leaving Paul alone. But Marianna appeared at his side suddenly, tapping him on the back.

"Entertaining yourself?" she asked. "The grill's almost ready, so grab those veggie burgers. You want another beer? How are you doing?"

Paul's energy always flagged around Marianna, as though there was only enough room for a limited amount of enthusiasm in any given place. "Great—thanks for inviting me."

"Ah, ah, I see—well, don't worry. I'm sure Julie will be here soon. She was just going to take a nap before she came over." Julie apparently worked as a legislative editor—long hours—and so apparently took naps.

Marianna ushered him into the house, her arm across his shoulders all the way. At times like this, he really wanted to love her, the way he'd wanted and failed to love everybody since the botany major. When he looked at trees, he imagined the botany major's hair and clothes shifting in unsettled air. But even that felt like nothing.

"You're going to love Julie," Marianna said, sitting on the counter and watching as Paul retrieved his food from the freezer. "That was some wedding, the one where I met her. Massive. Everybody's getting married, huh? I guess you'll be next."

"I haven't even met her yet," he said.

"I mean to whoever. It seems like everybody's almost there, approaching *final destination*."

"Whoa—that sounds kind of like death."

"No, no," she said, shaking her curls. "It's just where you can settle in, you know, and relax."

"Like Camelot," Paul said, testing it.

She jumped off the counter with energy, as though about to tousle his hair. "Camelot was destroyed, wasn't it? And they had to start over?" she said. "I'm talking about the *final* destination."

Outside, he put a couple of patties on the grill, trying to keep them separate from the meat without seeming like he cared. Ben clapped him on the back once, and said he'd never tried those things, but would have to someday.

"I have extras," Paul suggested.

"Not today, buddy," Ben said.

The smell of meat curled up among the charcoal smoke, and Paul had to admit to himself that it made his mouth water a little. He had not given up meat out of disgust or disinterest. So he stepped back a pace or two and ended up among a few people who worked with Ben at the magazine. They discussed intricate recipes for cold soups, thin cream sauces, and homemade polenta, each person looking at one another's hands as they pantomimed mincing, stirring, and the shape of exotic vegetables.

Paul found himself able to maintain his very minor role in the conversation with half his attention, and simultaneously tried to put a face to Julie, one less monstrous and more calm than the one inspired by Marianna's description. He did what he had often done, almost ritually, when he thought about a woman he had just met or was about to meet—he imagined himself ballroom dancing with her, both of them so tall (which made Julie easy to picture already, since supposedly she actually *was* tall), waltzing slowly but dramatically in formal clothes across a finished wooden floor. As they breathed one another in, their eyes went wide with excitement and recognition.

On the opposite end of things from that scene was his actual life. The night before, Paul had spent hours crawling through the Internet, looking for pornographic stories. Stories, not photos, because photos meant a victim, but stories could exist without real women. He'd started out looking at love stories by little kids at school sites—so innocent!—but then found himself gravitating toward sites by adults instead, and then pornography, collections of tall tales rife with misspellings, distended body parts, and hurried grammar.

Unexpectedly, they came in categories, categories that were fairly consistent across Web sites—fetishes, teenagers' first times, lesbians, and dozens and dozens about cheating wives. Those stories seemed to be in endless supply. Something fascinated people about unfaithful wives, and, in fact, it fascinated Paul, too. Perhaps the narrators, cuckolds masturbating from their hiding places, were impressive because they'd made desperation somehow satisfying. Paul came into a T-shirt, and went to bed with only sorrow left over.

He looked over at Marianna, whom he did not love, in the context of those Web sites. Perhaps Ben imagined her cheating when he fantasized. Maybe they even discussed it. Here, though, Ben's hand never left Marianna's back. Paul shook his head—he had been so long by himself he no longer knew the difference between ballroom dancing, pornography, and marriage. He wondered if that Max wasn't onto something.

He had not yet really met anyone else at the party by the time his dinner was ready—names washed over him, as his presumably did over others. Paul waited for Julie to show up, as though waiting for a train carrying an old friend, though she wasn't, of course. What else had Marianna told him about her? He got drunk as he thought about it. The mosquitoes found the barbecue and seemed to especially like the people working for the magazine, and Paul managed to feel some jealousy about even that. Twilight began, barely, to settle.

At last he returned to the cheese dip and the chips. The rhythm of it blended well with his mental image of ballroom dancing, and he became lost in reverie. Just then, Max reappeared, rubbing his scalp.

"Oh—I'd lost track of you," Paul said.

"Mm. Yes. I leave no tracks. Have you made any friends yet?"

"Not really," he said. Then he decided to confess something, as though via a sudden intimacy he could trap Max into friendship. "I'm waiting for this woman to show up. Marianna's setting me up."

"Setting you up? Isn't *that* a nice expression?" he said. "What's she supposed to be like?"

"Well, I guess big. Big, I was told, and imposing, and striking."

"Hm." His lips curled out in thought. "It sounds like your hostess is setting you up, all right."

"No, no—she's great, I think. Marianna raves about her. I'm looking forward to it. I haven't had a date in practically a year," he added in another burst.

"Ah ha!" Max shot a finger in the air. "You're doing the same thing you accused *me* of. You're just *between* things, aren't you? Take my advice—break the cycle."

"Huh."

"Anyway, I'm going," Max said. They shook hands again.

Marianna appeared at Paul's side. "Hey, hey," she said.

"Any word from Julie?" he asked. If he didn't meet her tonight, he might just end up at home gorging on unfaithful wives and feeling ashamed about it later. His picture of Julie now was elegant, and he'd had enough to drink that he would be fearless talking to her.

"Well. I'm not really sure," Marianna said, wrinkling her face into an apology. "You know what? She said if her nap went long she might not come, actually. I didn't want to tell you, but I guess she might just stay in bed."

"Oh," Paul said, concentrating on his facial muscles, not wanting to convey anything emotional.

Later, Paul wandered from group to group listlessly. Julie never did show up. Max, too, seemed to have left, and Paul had wanted to catch up with him. He had been thinking about Max, actually, ever since admitting all that stuff to him. On some level, he wanted the friendship he had bought with those words, or, if not, he wanted his words back.

In the end, Marianna walked Paul around front and gave him a hug for reassurance. "You'll meet another time. She's excited about it, I swear."

"Sure. Hey, is that guy Max your friend or Ben's?"

"Who?"

"The bald guy with the Speed Racer T-shirt," he said.

"The bald guy? Oh, you talked to him, too? Yeah, neither of us knows him—nobody does. He talked to a bunch of people, and everybody thought somebody else knew him. He just snuck in off the street and ate some of the food, I guess. Funny, huh?"

"Funny," Paul said, and they hugged again before he left, his face buried in her bouncy hair.

The smell of other grills filled the street, and Paul walked slowly at first to appreciate them.

Halfway down the block he saw a group standing in a driveway, talking loudly and drinking under artificial lights. He stopped completely to watch. They stood together, all turned inward as though the grill radiated a powerful magnetism. The driveway gave them borders, and none looked out toward the street.

And then he saw a bald man move among them, and out toward the edges, where he grabbed a handful of pretzels. Nobody saw him, and Paul started in that direction. But then Max had vanished again, disappearing behind some people, off toward other plumes of charcoal smoke, billowing up into the air.

The Movements of the Body

WHEN CATHY got to work, her breath was already a sharp, sweet mixture of whiskey and mouthwash. Her damp breath surrounded her. It washed over the receptionist, who would have to have been used to the smell but winced anyway, because of the strength of it. Cathy's breath filled the hallway in a vague but pervasive way as she walked back to her desk, aware of each one of her movements, consciously in control of all of them.

She exhaled once more as she arrived and dropped her bag against her cubicle wall. The drop sent a shudder through her desk, causing a framed picture to shake, and she reacted too vehemently, grabbing for it with both hands and thrusting it up into the air as though holding a baby snatched away from the brink of a great fall. Shaken, Cathy sank into her chair, holding the picture. It was a picture of her grandson, her daughter's only child. She felt lingering shock.

"Good morning," said Jean, the woman across the low cubicle partition from her. It was a feeble sound, this *Good morning*, a sort of hesitant breeze through reeds. This was the woman who, at work, breathed only Cathy's strange air, the mix of alcohol and mouthwash across from the other desk, every day. During lunch, Jean ate her food with tight lips and the anxious chewing of a guinea pig, hunched over her food.

Cathy was startled by the greeting, and felt the gates open. "Yes—good morning," she said brightly. "You know, I was walking from the subway station and after a block I took off my gloves. It's really not as cold as it was. I mean, it's still winter, but it's really not that bad. It could be a lot worse."

Jean huddled in on herself instinctively. "Oh—it's still too cold for me," she said, with a little laugh.

Cathy laughed in an abrupt kind of way. "No, I know you're not a winter person. And we've got a while longer with it, too, I think—that's what they're saying. Not that they ever know what they're talking about, of course. You can never count on what they tell you. You just can't." She forced her head down toward her computer monitor, turned on her machine. She wanted to stop talking. She focused as hard as possible on the screen and willed silence to settle in around her. As the monitor flashed back and forth from black in its efforts, she could off and on see a foggy idea of her reflection. Cathy's ever softer face seemed as though it had been tenderized over many years by determined force. She looked away, looked back at the picture of her eight-year-old grandson, still in her hand.

Drey was not like other kids in this generation, who could at a moment's notice transform themselves into prepackaged, frozen images of cuteness for the camera. In this photo, taken a couple of years ago, Drey looked like he always did—vaguely suspicious, every peek from under black bangs a sideways peek.

That's how he'd looked at his mother last night when Cathy brought him back to his house and they found her asleep, sprawled face-up on the couch under a blanket. Her daughter's naked shoulders were free of the blanket, her naked leg sneaking out from another side to let her foot dangle loosely against the floor. There was, Cathy saw in the light provided only by a muted television, the bright wrapper of a condom just under the couch. Drey didn't look right at her, but kept on going to his room, watching his mother sideways and mumbling "G'bye Gramma" on the way. The sight of his determined back made Cathy almost stagger on her feet.

She'd had a moment where she thought she might grab her daughter around the neck and yank her upright, yank her by her neck back into awakeness. Instead she slowly walked through the room, back and forth, picking up the toppled empty beer bottles and the pizza box, folding the dirty clothes into a pile, including a man's undershirt. Then she just sat on the coffee table by her daughter to watch her face. Lisa was almost a pretty girl, she thought, would be if her teeth weren't yellowed, if her face wasn't a little puffy and pasty, like Cathy's, if the red dye in her hair was a little less angry. As it was, Lisa looked like someone always suffering through trying emotions.

Before she left, Cathy checked in on Drey, and in his room saw the whites of his eyes gleaming, though he said nothing when she asked if he was awake.

"How was your weekend?" Jean asked now, her voice low and hesitant. Cathy returned to the scene around her with a jolt, almost as if she had been away physically somehow.

"Not bad," she said. "Not bad at all, really. I saw my grandson, Drey. We spent a whole day together, which was really special, and I don't always get to do that. I love to see my grandson," she said, and then she turned back to her computer, which was just about ready to go.

Throughout the morning, Jean asked Cathy questions about the surveys they were compiling. They had been there the same length of time, but over time they had both come to regard Cathy as the authority on their work. Jean had a way of forgetting what to do when the companies they were supposed to contact said they weren't interested in surveys, or if they said they had no marketing director, or if there were two entries in the Excel file under the same name, and a lot of other things, too. Cathy's elaborate discourses on these things filled the air that morning.

Just before lunch, Cathy's sister Pat called from their mother's place, because their mother couldn't find the shoes she wanted and so was refusing to go to her doctor's appointment. This was the thing about having gotten pregnant young, and her daughter having gotten pregnant young—there was so much family all around her.

"I've tried to get her to wear the other black ones," Pat said. Cathy could hear the smoke in her breath.

"It has to be the *right* shoes," came the sound of her mother's voice from the background, from somewhere near Pat. Her voice was drunk.

"It's not about the shoes," Cathy said. "It's about the doctor. She doesn't want to go to the doctor, but she has to go. You know you've got to get her to go."

"Look," Pat said, "I'm taking a day off from work to do this—"

"I know. I know. I understand that perfectly. I'm just saying that she has to go to the doctor, with whatever shoes she has, but she's got to go. Do you see what I mean?"

"You can't make me wear those," came her mother's voice again. Pat sighed smoke into the receiver.

As always, after the call, Jean acted as though she hadn't heard a word. She said, "Are we—are we still going out for a drink after work?"

Cathy felt a little stunned, and felt she was noticing herself talk rather than making it happen. "Sure, definitely," she said. "I think we'll go to this little place just three blocks down. It's not so expensive as these other places, those places where the rich guys go for their martini lunches. I can't believe what some places charge around here. You know, I think I'll go get some lunch myself."

In a stall in the bathroom she pulled out a little flask-sized glass bottle of whiskey and a plastic bottle of mouthwash and squeezed them both in her hands.

Cathy had no appetite for lunch and once she was outside she walked in a nearly random direction for several blocks. The buildings were towers and the sky was remote. She turned onto a side street, one lined with stalls aimed to attract the tourists. Still, she stopped at one and looked at the tiny stuffed animals wearing NYPD T-shirts. For a minute she thought about getting one as a spontaneous gift for Drey, but then decided he was already past the stage where he would enjoy it. He was a very serious kid. He didn't tell eight-year-old-style jokes. He avoided sports. He didn't care if he ever had dessert or not. She touched the fur on one bear and then walked off again.

In the bathroom of a deli nearby she finished the bottle of

whiskey. She knew how to achieve the right balance, to remain in control while limiting her focus to the movements of her body, or whatever else was immediate. The taste of mouthwash was for her the taste of balance as well.

That afternoon they dealt with a problem in the database, which was, for some reason, adding zeros to all the numbers in most of the records, and not always at the ends of the numbers. Jean was already half-panicked about it by the time Cathy got back from lunch. She leaned over Jean's shoulder and they watched the screen together. Cathy was aware of the smell of her breath, but more aware of the problem with the zeros. It wasn't happening in every record—but there had to be a pattern somewhere. She looked at the rank they'd assigned the companies, the location of the main office, the place in the alphabet. There was no pattern. She spent the afternoon on the phone with the computer people downstairs, trying to figure it out, and Jean worked on something else.

She interrupted herself late in the day to call her mother, who answered after seven rings. Cathy wondered what had happened to the answering machine.

"What?" her mother said when she picked up the phone. "What?"

"Mom, it's Cathy. Did you go to the doctor today?"

"What? Cathy? No, no, I didn't go to the doctor today." She sounded much more drunk than she had earlier.

Cathy sighed. "Is Pat still there?"

"Pat? You want to know about Pat? I sent her home. I don't need Pat around here."

"Mom, you had an appointment with the doctor. This is

serious. You know this is serious. We talked about this appointment."

"I don't need Pat around here," she said.

"Mom, why are you doing this?" Cathy said, and then she heard the sounds of her mother crying and punctuating her crying with coughing. Her mother all of a sudden couldn't even talk.

"Mom? Mom? It's okay, Mom. It's going to be fine. We'll make another appointment, Mom."

"Do you know what it's like for your children to try to raise you?" she said, still crying, but less. "That's how I feel. Do you know what that's like?"

"Okay, Mom."

Soon after that they hung up. Jean was working hard on her project, her face low over her keyboard. Cathy went to the bathroom and then came back. She could hardly make sense of her computer screen, no matter how she stared at it. She called her daughter. Lisa was home, not out looking for work.

"I was hoping I wouldn't find you at home," she said. "I really was hoping not to."

"Mom," Lisa said, her voice like a person just waking up, "not now, okay?"

"Have you been crying about something?"

"No," Lisa said. "Don't worry about it. I'm going to go get a job. I'm going to do it."

"I know," Cathy said.

"Thanks for watching Drey yesterday," Lisa said. "I think he had a really good time."

Cathy put her hand over her mouth and felt her face trembling. She stayed as still as possible, hand over mouth, until she was calm, and then she got off the phone as fast as she could.

After one more pass over the database, Cathy knocked on her boss's doorframe. He was inside the office with his chin in his hand, staring at his computer screen. He didn't look at her as she stood there at the open door.

"God dammit," he said. "These fucking, fucking, fucking computers." Very suddenly he struck a key on his keyboard, three times, hard. Cathy jumped slightly, and just started talking.

"Not working, is it?" she said. "These things can be so frustrating. You never know exactly what's going on with a computer. I mean, obviously to some extent you have to, but still—I just—we've really been struggling all day—all afternoon—with the same kind of thing. You know—"

"Cathy," he said, turning his eyes on her and throwing a hand up. "You know what? I'm real busy. Could you just tell me what's going on with the database?"

Cathy froze, and opened her mouth once, and closed it. She shook her head a little, and tried again. "We're working on it," she said. "We're working on it. The computer people were trying to help me, but we still don't—"

He put his hand up again. "Okay," he said. "Fine. Let me get back to this."

When he took his eyes off her she felt as though she was suddenly able to breathe again. She backed out of his office silently, almost gasping.

After work, Cathy and Jean walked down a few blocks to Clancy's, a place Cathy had been on her lunch breaks before. It was colder than it had been at lunch, and it was full night as they walked, the sun having set officially hours ago, and even earlier having fallen behind all these buildings.

"I'm glad we're doing this?" Jean said, almost inaudible over the traffic, the end of her statement an inadvertent question.

"Me, too," Cathy said. "I don't know why we've waited so long, really." They had never before spent time together outside of work. But she was tired of talking. Her head hurt. There was something so strange about drinking socially. She just wanted her next drink. She didn't want the bartender there to make a big show of recognizing her, but she wanted to see him because she wanted her next drink. They walked quietly through the cold, Jean buried in her heavy coat, and the world around them was loud with buses and taxis and all their horns.

Clancy's was quiet, too, with only a few diehards at the bar, one of them talking softly to the bartender, the TV mumbling to itself. It was only Monday evening. Cathy was used to thinking of all the nights in the same way.

They ordered drinks at the bar, Jean a white wine and Cathy a gin and tonic, and then sat at a little table far from the door. Jean was terrified of the possibility of cold drafts.

"So," Cathy said after swallowing a good portion of what was in her glass. They made them strong at Clancy's.

Jean laughed nervously. She often laughed almost as a show of surprise, or as an apology. She laughed often when she talked.

"Boy, that database is murder," Cathy said at last. "I mean, we really wrestled with that database all day, and even when I thought we had it, we didn't have it. They can be so tricky."

Jean smiled, said, "I think so." For a few minutes then, they talked about work. It was a natural thing to do, and not too hard. Cathy ordered another drink, while Jean continued to work on her first. It wasn't so bad to be here. The headache was fading a little.

"I don't know why we waited so long to do this," Cathy said.

"Me either," Jean said, and then she laughed. "Usually I just go home after work and watch TV."

"I never could get into television much," Cathy said. "I just couldn't get the interest going. All those sitcoms and game shows and everything. They never appealed to me. You know what? I used to read a lot instead. I loved to read."

"Do you still? Read?"

Cathy focused on her. She was controlling what she focused on. "Not really," she said.

"What do you do?"

Cathy thought about that, and drank her glass empty, and thought more. She spent a lot of time on the phone. Too much. She sat by the window in her kitchen.

"Yesterday my grandson and I went to the park," Cathy said.

"The park? But it's so cold."

Cathy laughed, a full laugh. "Kids don't feel the cold." Or drunks, either, she thought, but not unhappily. It was a good thing to not feel the cold. "He ran all around with some other kids, and there was a dog, too. This really huge dog." She held her hands out and then dropped them before they reached the size of the dog. She was picturing the bright blue eyes of the dog, which had looked like a wolf. Like a purebred wolf. Her grandson's eyes were blue, too, though not that blue. She knew that many people started out with blue eyes but then lost them. She thought her grandson might be too old to lose them.

"You stopped talking," Jean said quietly.

"What? Oh—I was just thinking about Drey."

"Drey?"

"My grandson."

"Oh," Jean said. "I never knew his name."

Cathy stared at her, pursing her lips, breathing through her nose.

"Um, is he your daughter's son, or your son's son?"

Cathy stared for another minute. She focused all of her energy on that, and not on thinking. Jean's face seemed to be unstable, shifting.

"Cathy?"

"What? Sorry. Right. He's my daughter's son. I only have a daughter. I thought I'd said that before. And his name. I thought I must have mentioned that, but I guess I didn't. I must not have."

"Cathy?" Jean looked worried.

"Listen," Cathy said. "I'll be right back, okay?" She drank deeply again and then got up to go to the bathroom. She looked back once as she walked. Jean was steadily shredding her napkin, her mouth wide open.

Inside, Cathy just stared at the mirror. She was feeling something like a kind of fury, something that would be bright orange or red if you could see it. She wanted to smash the mirror. She wanted to smash the mirror and with a bleeding hand carry out the biggest shard and put it right on the table in front of Jean.

Cathy turned on the faucet, cold, and caught some water in her hand, brought it to her mouth, to her face generally, just to see what it would taste like in this intensity of feeling. But it didn't taste like anything. It was the same in her mouth as anywhere else on her face. She pulled her face back up to the mirror and watched it drip, and when she opened her mouth, she watched the water empty out of that, too. And then she went back out to sit down with Jean.

Bridesmaid

"ARE YOU here alone?"

This is now. I'm being asked this now. Standing next to my table is a woman, a skinny woman with somewhat curly dirty-blond hair all the way down her back, a black silk sleeveless shirt on. She looks polished, done-up, though perhaps look at the thin lips, the bony bump in the nose, the skinny neck—a bit awkward, too.

It's amazing to see her so clearly, through the darkness of the bar and more importantly all the fog in me, but it's because she's so absolutely *right here*, focused right on me, smiling with lots of teeth.

I suddenly feel that I am taking a long time to answer. So long, in fact, that I let it stretch on a little longer, just to see if I can, just to watch the moment grow. I take in her cheekbones, her freckled shoulders, her dangly black-ball earrings.

"Pretty much," I say, and it must not have been much of a delay after all, because she doesn't seem bothered.

"Pretty much?" she says, knotting her hands together. "Does that mean no?"

"Oh, no," I say. "I'm sorry. I am. I'm by myself."

"Those are my friends," she says, pointing off to the side. I turn, the bar a blur around my head, and see a group of four or five—it's four—women there, just a few yards away. They all immediately wave wildly at me, as startling as a dozen pigeons bursting into flight right at my feet. Like the woman by me, they're skinny, dressed nicely, young professionals, but one with straight black hair and sharp red lips is wearing a veil, pulled back off her face. This shocks me—I see Deborah in that wedding dress, feel my fingers in the veil, me getting ready to pull it up and find out who I've got in front of me. I think about us circling each other, Deborah's unreadable face. As these women wave and laugh, my right hand by instinct jumps to my left under the table, touches my wedding band.

"Gina's getting married tomorrow night."

I turn back to this woman, in a bit of shock, worrying my ring. "To a nice guy?" I ask.

She sighs and awkwardly asks if she can sit down. There's another stool there, it seems. I wave her onto it, completely off my guard, still worrying my finger but unable through my haze to really think clearly about that.

"I wish I liked him better," she says. She has an accent, all the vowels really two vowels in one, stretching words out around them. "He's a good guy, I guess. Just not a communicator, you know? He doesn't express himself."

"You mean say 'I love you,' things like that?"

"Exactly!" she says gratefully, before shrinking back into guilt. "Don't tell Gina."

I look over to the table, catch a flash of veil, turn back. This woman in front of me is a little drunk herself. We're on the same plane of existence. And when I look at her, I'm completely absorbed into her powerful focus. It's as though her intensity knocks out my peripheral vision.

"Are you the maid of honor?" I ask.

She wrinkles her nose, shakes her head. "A bridesmaid," she says, seeming to apologize—not for correcting me, but for carrying less prestige than I might have wanted.

"Still, that's great." I don't know what I'm talking about, still feeling my ring finger and trying to wonder articulately what's happening.

"What about you?" she says.

"What about me?" I feel like this woman is from another planet, but that maybe I am, too.

"What are you doing here alone, I mean?"

I stare at my beer as though looking for a crib sheet. The glass is, as they say, half full.

"I don't know," I say, very seriously. "I guess I'm just out."

"No girlfriend?"

That's an easy one, if I take her words literally. "No, no." No wife, either, actually. Not living.

She smiles again, big. "I'm single, too," she says, and leans her cheek on her palm, a wistful look on her face.

I feel a burst, a rush of gratitude for this woman, for her generosity, for her being so aggressive and honest. Whatever planet she's from, it is a giving place, softhearted.

"You're great," I say without thinking, but really meaning it right now.

Her face opens up as though this is her very first compliment, and as though the experience is everything she'd ever imagined it would be.

It's really something, getting to know someone while not telling her the one enormous fact that dominates my life, or any of the surrounding facts. Not giving her any of my old existence, I guess. Part of the secret, of course, is asking a lot of questions.

Turns out she's a corporate manager at First Union. "Everyone's a manager at a bank," she says. "Even the janitor, probably." She is anxious to not put me off. She's also originally from Maryland, outside Baltimore, is therefore a baseball fan, and was raised vaguely Protestant. "Presbyterian, maybe? Does that sound right?" she says. I shrug, *I don't know from Protestants.* "Well, I still do Christmas and everything, but I'm not religious. Spiritual, maybe." She has two sisters (like me), divorced parents (also like me), grew up wanting to own a dog but never has (like me all the way?). Majored in psychology. All sorts of things that seem very normal to me.

At the same time, despite my great efforts, I'm hearing a parallel monologue. My mind is partly three years back, on my first date with Deborah, out at the White Dog Café in West Philly, and she's giving me the same kind of information. She works as a program director for Yisrael Echad, arranging for kids to spend summers and spring breaks and whole school years in Israel. *Program director?* she says. *More like butler, maid, and chauffeur.* Though she loves it, actually. She's originally from Philadelphia, is therefore a fan of all the big four sports, and was raised increasingly Jewishly. *My mother discovered Judaism late,* she says. She has no siblings, parents still married and absolutely in love, never wanted a pet. Majored in Jewish and Middle Eastern studies. I *have* to get her out of my head. All that those thoughts do is abuse me.

These two monologues, interrupted by brief interjections

from me, go on side by side, despite all my efforts to shut one out and focus on the other. Here this woman is, in front of me, not dead, and not planning to leave me, dead or alive. I have my ring-bearing hand under the table.

"You're a great listener," she says, leaning in pretty close to me. This leaning fills my ribcage with thunder, or maybe makes it feel like a boxer is working my heart like the small bag. It's an awful, terrifying feeling, absolutely intolerable. But then she leans away again, and I grab my glass, fill my mouth with beer. "Sorry," she says.

"No, no. No, really." I'm very drunk, can't quite put a sentence together. "Thanks for saying I'm a listener." She smiles, uncertainly, and this eggs me on. I raise my glass. "To listening!"

Her face opens up again, and she clinks her beer against mine. We sit quietly, but she looks a little roused. I remember this look. Before I met Deborah, a lot of women looked at me that way— as though they'd found what they'd been looking for. And me too, truly—they were all possibilities I wanted so much to save me that I gave *them* faith. Then, at three months, when I'd become scared, frustrated, bored, or disappointed, that look would become betrayal, the kind of total betrayal that can only happen when you've been made to believe in something against your will, only to have it turn up false in the very hands of the person who made you believe. Deborah was tougher. She never gave me the look I'm getting now.

"I think you're great, too," she says, leaning in—thunder, punches—and out again.

I glance over at her friends while we continue talking and drinking. They're looking away, but not pointedly—they've gone on without one of their bridesmaids. And here I am with her, on what I realize is becoming a kind of date. We have given our basic personal information, or at least she has, and now we talk about our attitudes, our opinions. Books, movies—she's seen and read everything that everybody is seeing and reading.

I nod, thinking that this finding-out conversation is much less important to me than I want it to be. I find myself agreeing with her when she changes the topic—says that people are scared to take risks in life—but I do it passionlessly. So am I one of those guys, now, who decides the woman meets his standards just by a smile or nice eyes or, worse yet, the curve of her breasts, no personality necessary? Yet she has such an earnestness about her, and I think that's what grabs me more than anything. Or maybe it's that look she gives me. I love being liked in this bar tonight.

"I think people *are* afraid," I say. "I mean, everybody is. It's just about who wants to run away from the fear, and who wants to walk toward it."

She pulls some curls from her face as if to show me her gratitude. "Yeah," she says, leaning in again. The pounding and trembling are intolerable.

"Do you think you could ever love someone as much as you love your own life?" I ask, so quietly.

"Are you kidding?" she says, still close to me. "That's easy. Who couldn't do that?"

I put my hands in her hair on either side, pull her face toward me, even though it would maybe have even gotten here without my help, and we kiss. It is a voracious, feral kiss, as though we're trying to get through each other, with tongues and lips and teeth. I am breathing very hard when we separate.

"I think you really should walk me home now," she says.

She lives very close by, though in my drunken, weaving state, I don't quite follow the route. We also stop every few yards and fly at one another, push each other up against cars, signposts, buildings, gnawing and licking and breathing.

When we get to her place, on the second floor, I don't see it. She doesn't even turn the lights on, but pulls me forcefully around what must be furniture, into a different dark room, and onto a high, soft bed. We are ferocious, chewing our clothes off, my hand squeezing her shoulders and her buttocks hard, her fingers pushing new and old bruises deep into my back. There is even the tiny taste of blood at the corner of my lip, one of us has bitten through skin there, and our limbs try to lock in the tightest possible way. I stretch her nipples with my lips, she pulls at my testicles, grasps my already-wet erection. I try to go down on her, haven't done this with any woman besides Deborah in so long that it feels like a completely different thing, like a thing I've only heard about, but you can't just hear about these things, I'm terrible, awkward, and she grabs my head with her hands, pushes my face hard against her for a second, and then she forces me up, reaches into a drawer, hands me the cold foil square, and with the condom on I'm inside her so fast, and this is different, too, but good, so unstoppable, so rough, she's screaming at me, I'm screaming at her, too raw to even feel love or hate, just *fucking* until it finally catches me, by surprise, swooping down and bursting open inside me like the birth of a new sun.

In the morning I see her apartment.

She is sleeping, and I'm just barely sliding awake in the low light of the bedroom—she has heavy shades—feeling the pain from my sobering head, the bruises from last night, even on my penis, which maybe she even bit, and I'm looking around. The first feeling, surprisingly, is not a mistaken feeling that I'm waking up in my apartment, our apartment. Deborah always kept the shades up, for one, so that many mornings I began to wake up before any alarm, awash in agitating light. Here it's not like that at all, and as I look at the clock I see it's later than I might expect. Maybe the alcohol kept me out.

So the first feeling isn't familiarity, in any case. It's a brutal kind of shock, and this I blame on the lost alcohol for sure. Now I can't make myself be oblivious. I am thrown into the ice-water cold of a morning in this apartment belonging to a stranger, a naked woman at my side, a punishment wrinkling the sheets, a judgment stretched out on her right side, facing away from me, one hand up under her pillow, the other down on top of that first arm, so that she's almost curled into a prayer, and I realize I'm sitting straight up in this room, on this bed, naked all the way down. The hangover pulses once, enormously, in my brain.

And so then, to calm myself, I take the bedroom in. I look around, at the large framed Ansel Adams crashing surf photo over the bed, and the valances on the windows, and the cloth runner on the bureau, spotted with small statuettes that might be animals or children. And the hairbrushes on the bureau, the clock radio next to the book—the one about the small New England town everyone's reading—on the nightstand. The thick carpets. The clothes looking like dead forms thrown here and there, but only ours, from last night. The woman.

I get up carefully, desperate not to wake her and yet needing to not be on that still bed. My pants, an undershirt I find easily enough, but instead of rooting around for the rest, I just step out of the room, my head booming loud enough to shatter her sleep, and I just want to be in some other part of the apartment. In the back of my mind, I'm hearing *hair of the dog, hair of the dog.*

It's a small place—a one-bedroom with a little living room full of small, comfy-type cute furniture. I run my hand along the back of the loveseat, think the word *loveseat,* see my ring shine dully, yank my hand away. I go into the kitchen, and open the fridge, stunned to find myself beer-hunting. *Hair of the dog, hair of the dog.* It's nearly empty in there, no beer, and not much else. Mostly there are condiments—mustards and low-cal mayonnaise and honey. I think the work *honey* and another pulse of blood batters my brain.

"Oh, good," she says behind me. I actually fall down from my squat as I turn, I'm so startled. I spin right to the ground.

"I thought you left," she says, looking like someone who's lost six or seven that way. She's in a silk bathrobe, maybe peach, her curly hair flopping down all over.

"No," I say. "No, I didn't leave."

"Yeah, I guess not."

"Right. No, I didn't."

The fridge air chills my back as she looks down at me, arms folded across her chest. Neither of us is naked, yet neither of us can not be.

"So hi," she says. Her voice is self-consciously cute, as though she's trying to soften the situation.

"Right. Hi."

"Whatcha looking for?"

I breathe in and out. We haven't moved. For some reason I tell her the truth. "Beer, I guess."

"Hair of the dog," she says, and it makes me reel. I can't quite stand her speaking my thoughts aloud. I don't manage a response.

"I don't keep any around the house," she says guiltily. "Calories."

Her embarrassment, her apology for not providing me with alcohol this early in the morning, me, who is some stranger she met in a bar and—she must now be realizing—is a bad mistake, fills me with shame, a shame that weighs a hundred pounds. If I was not already on the floor, I'd sink to it now. "It's okay," I say. "I don't really want any."

"I think I'm going to take a shower," she says. "Will you be here when I get out?"

"Yes," I say before thinking.

"Good." She gives a little wave and disappears around the corner. It's as though she really does disappear, sinking back into the darkness.

I don't know why I told her I'd still be here. I want to leave without saying a word, leaving so completely and secretly that I not only leave no trace, I leave no memory—I leave her the sense that *maybe* something happened last night, but probably not. And I want this place to slide off me so gently that the same thing happens to my own memory. And so as I hear the water begin running I go back to the bedroom, snap on the lights, and grab all my clothes.

This is a suit, a suit I've been wearing since the funeral, thirty-six hours straight now, rumpled and heavy with sweat and dirt. Soon enough I will look homeless wearing this. But I put on this overworn suit, or at least the dress shirt, throwing the jacket over my arm at first and then slinging it onto the bed and then yanking it off and dropping it on—there are no chairs in this bedroom— the night table. Yet what I can't find, not on the open carpet, not among the sheets or comforter, which I only touch with the tips of my fingers despite how stupid it makes me feel, not under the bed or dresser, are my underpants. They're completely gone. I'm loose in my pants, and horrified. Leaving my underpants is leaving the surest sign I've been here. I keep searching. "God, God, Deborah," I say to myself, over and over. "God, Deborah, God. I'm sorry." I feel the threat of tears beating on the inside of my storm windows.

Eventually I give up looking. They're gone, somehow gone, and she'll be out of the shower soon. Already exhausted, as though I haven't slept at all, I sit against the bathroom door in my suit, knees up to chest, feeling the rush of the water just in the door's gentle vibration. I don't know what I'm going to do, and I so much don't know that I keep sitting there, looking out in her living room with all the furniture designed to make one person comfortable while always inviting the possibility of a second person in. I decide it's best to leave, but as I get up the water stops, and that freezes me, even though there's still plenty of time to get out of there. I stand as though waiting in the living room for my date to the prom. I could still go.

Then the door opens, and she's in her robe again, hair up and wet, and she's startled to see me right there. She does look regal, hair up and robed in silk. She is an attractive woman. I feel—

She comes toward me, looking sad and awkward and guilty. "Listen," she says, as though about to say something to clear all this up, but then she's got a hand on my chest, is kissing me, more gently than last night, so hopeful. Then she pulls back. "I'll be right out," she says, fading back toward the bedroom.

What's inexcusable is not the kiss—it's the erection that reaches up, loose in my pants.

I bolt—loud, clumsy, too obvious to be missed, even through the closed bedroom door. On the stairs, I'm tumbling stone.

Nothing Ever Happens
in White America

THE SNOW started up just about an hour outside of Madison, when all signs of the little city were long gone and the highway was swinging through moderate hills. At first, the only thing holding onto it was the grass, but it started to build up over the miles, clinging to old patches of stubborn ice that probably had been there since November. I hadn't spent much time outside the city since I moved to the area, yet I imagined northern Wisconsin to always be frozen, even in the summer. Whenever I got back to Atlanta, my grandmother was amazed by my pictures—whether I was alone in a crowd of white people or up against a snowdrift, she said I looked like one black ant in a sugar bowl.

Matt had the radio on scan, and it was chasing across the dial, trying to find something interesting to cover the road noise, picking through the bursts of sound among the silent lapses. I suddenly noticed it when I realized I was beginning to be able to piece the various songs together just by hearing tiny parts of them over and over.

"You want me to turn this off?" I offered.

"Oh, yeah—maybe you could put in a tape or something," he said, turning his bright eyes on me. He played with a lock of light brown hair behind his ear. "I can never settle on anything."

He seemed excited. I guess he'd been on this route a million times, riding up to his parents' cabin on weekends and holidays and for vacations, but this weekend seemed to make it new again. I was impressed with him, bringing a black man up north for a long weekend in his parents' hot tub, and us knowing each other just a couple of weeks. At this point in a relationship, I was usually more cautious than that—so nervous I couldn't stand still long enough to count the buttons on the man's shirt. We hadn't even been very intimate yet. Then, the thought of rural Wisconsin made me anxious, too—my black friends in Madison had told me to be wary.

About halfway through the trip, I got hungry.

"We'd better stop, then," Matt said. "We're not going to reach the cabin for hours."

"My first shot at real Wisconsin culture."

"Prepare to be underwhelmed," Matt said.

We stopped off at a gas station to fill up the tank and to pick up some travel food, on the order of beef jerky or corn nuts. I felt like I was dressed perfectly to fit in, wearing a baseball cap with the high trucker's front and a flannel shirt with jeans. I thought maybe folks around there would assume I was local. In any case, the woman in the little gas station market didn't react much to me one way or the other.

"Marcus—what do you think?" Matt asked me, a pair of round-lens sunglasses on, holding the price tag up and away from his nose in an attempt to see what he looked like in the mirror. They looked good on him, matched his tendency toward

European-style button-down shirts and dark vests. He was so cute that I felt a certain hope about things.

By the time we got to Eagle River, a little town without many bright lights, it was fully dark. The snow had dropped off completely, having left its marks on top of the old drifts and a permanent icy crust covering the town streets. We drove through, up and down the quiet main street, just so I could see it, and then turned the car around. We were going to the White Stag Inn, a steak place we'd passed on the way in. Although I wasn't much for red meat, I felt it would only be right to eat a steak in such a place, just as it would be to have curry in India.

The place was full, and everybody seemed like regulars; at each table they sat slightly turned away from one another without talking, as though it was their dining room at home. Everybody in there seemed to be heterosexual couples and families. They were as white as the day is long, and most of the men had rounded, content bellies. Still, though we stuck out, they put us at a prominent table, in plain view of the open grill where the chefs were preparing the steaks. As it turned out, the menu had little more to it than a wide variety of steaks. There were several sizes and several cuts, and a couple of other meat options, like pork and even chicken, for the weakest among us. I was determined to have a big slice of cow, cooked hard.

"Ever been in a place quite like this?" Matt asked. I hadn't. "I envy how you grew up—the one time I went to Atlanta, I liked it so much, it was painful afterwards to come back to Wisconsin."

The only time Matt had ever lived away from the state for any length of time was during a vaguely mentioned but apparently recent long-term relationship in northern Illinois. Now he said

49

he wanted to get out again, see a little more of the "real world." "That's what's great about you," he said—the fact that I'd grown up all-black in an all-black neighborhood, in a school with Vietnamese kids, whites, Cubans, who knows what-all. And hey—I was fascinated by him, too.

When the salad arrived, he was grinning, because he knew what was coming. "You're not going to believe this," he said, as the huge bowl was placed at the center of the table and complemented by three smaller dishes holding colorful dressings. The wooden bowl was full of iceberg lettuce, heads of iceberg sliced neatly into quarters, and that was the entire salad—just a pile of dense, watery green wedges that we were to break into pieces into our own bowls. Matt was clearly excited, hoping I'd never seen anything like it. I hadn't.

He had a way of brightening visibly when he wanted to share something. It was the way he looked when he first held my hand in public, as we walked between paintings in the Elvehjem Museum and arrived in front of the sole Georgia O'Keefe. It was a flowerless-vase painting that looked like nothing else of hers I'd ever encountered, yet it had been his first experience with her.

He told me about the dinners he and his family used to have at this place. On these vacations there was an implicit agreement not to discuss issues of sensible diet. Matt's favorite part had always been the salad, because even as a kid he could sense that it was strange—combining the dressings, and the way the wedge of iceberg lettuce rocked in his bowl like a slice of melon.

He asked me where I went on vacations as a child.

"Well, the furthest we ever went, maybe the best trip we ever took, was up into North Carolina, Kill Devil Hills and Nags Head.

We traveled all around, stopping in motels with pools and along the beach." He stared at me intently, chin in hand, as if to memorize every detail. "I think we were moving from bargain to bargain. My dad was always looking for the best deal, just for the sport of it. We stayed in some terrible places, I guess, though I don't remember that. I remember that we were able to eat whatever we wanted, maybe just like you, and that I walked around the hotel room with my hand stuffed in a can of Pringles, chewing and happy as I could be."

My parents hardly ever talked to me now that I'd come out, except for some infrequent contact by my mother. Occasionally there was a phone call close to the holidays or my birthday, but not so close that we had to discuss why they weren't encouraging me to come home anymore. On the rare occasion we talked, she never asked me anything about my social life, and I knew she was afraid to.

When the steak arrived, I tore into it eagerly and genuinely enjoyed myself. I caught the waitress staring at us hopefully until she determined that I liked the meal, at which point she smiled broadly, the proud hostess, and moved to another room. I wondered what she thought of us. Matt had been looking at me the same way, trying to gauge my reaction before deciding upon his own, or just trying to see how my food tasted to me by looking into my eyes and watching the way my closed lips moved as I chewed.

The living room in Matt's cabin had two sliding-glass doors facing south toward a lake, and light had already muscled its way in to fill every corner of the space by nine the next morning. I was sitting with a mug of coffee and skimming a copy of *Jaws* that had been sitting on the mantelpiece over the fireplace, among a bunch of other books that his family had decided weren't important enough to ever take back with them. It was warm for a cabin —I'd been imagining something slapdash and full of holes, not because Matt seemed poor, but because I'd always imagined cabins in the woods to be that way. This even though I'd known that this one had a hot tub. (As soon as I'd gotten out of bed that morning, leaving him asleep, I opened my journal and made a heading called "firsts." I wrote under it, along with a description of the salad from the night before, "kissing and cuddling in a hot tub—slippery.")

There were pictures all over the living room, some people I thought I could identify just from having heard about them, like his grandfather, who was hairy, and his sister, who had glasses and who was the same height as him in all the pictures. But then I thought I found a second sister or a cousin, a beautiful woman with curly, milk-chocolate hair and lots of teeth. In one picture, I was surprised by how closely this woman and Matt were holding one another, and I spotted the Chicago Art Institute behind them.

I had a powerful gnawing feeling in my stomach by the time he got up, shuffling into the living room in boxer shorts.

"Breakfast?" I asked.

"And good morning to you," he said, landing on top of me on the couch. He was skinny, but something in him weighed a lot—maybe the steak from the night before.

"Clothes," I said, tousling his pre-tousled hair and kissing his forehead once, "Clothes time and breakfast time."

"Oh, all right," he said, and sat up again.

"I'm just fooling around—take your time. I can hold off. I've been chewing my nails all morning so that's been keeping my appetite down."

"No, no," he said, moving back toward the bedroom door, "I'll shower later. I want to keep smelling like you for a while. Hey—by the way, sorry about pooping out a little last night."

I smiled and tried to radiate forgiveness. I wasn't dwelling on it, though it had been disappointing—he'd had a lot of wine in the hot tub, and then claimed to not feel well by the time we were in bed. Something about it had felt like an excuse. "That's okay, Matt," I said, and he smiled gratefully, getting up to leave.

"Hey, one thing I'm curious about. What's the name of that old girlfriend of yours?" I teased, pointing at the picture in front of the Art Institute and expecting him to say she was a cousin. "She's beautiful."

Matt's face flushed a little. "Oh. That's my ex-wife Allison," he said, and disappeared out of sight. I heard the bedroom door shut.

There was a restaurant in town named the Copper Kettle where, filling several pages of the menu, there were people listed who had eaten record numbers of pancakes. The minimum to make the menu seemed to be ten pancakes, which had been achieved by a huge number of people, and the records ranged all the way up to fifteen. There were only a couple of names under that one.

"Don't try," Matt said. "They're not silver dollar pancakes, you know, and after my uncle made the list, he was sick for a couple of hours. There's a tablespoon of butter on each one, I think."

"Wow."

We had not returned to the topic of his ex-wife. He was allowed, I'd reminded myself, to have a past.

"Like another planet, huh?"

"Maybe," I shrugged, looking around the dark room, low ceilings, which were already a little cloudy with cigarette smoke. The place was very wooden. "But it's kind of exciting." I *was* excited, having never seen any place quite like this. I half-wanted to try to eat ten pancakes just to squeak into the menu under the wire.

"You must be crazy. When I think of what these people are missing in terms of culture . . ."

"Well, that's not true, is it? They've got, what, German culture, right? And Scandinavian culture? Don't they make fudge or something here?"

"You know what I mean," he said, and was distracted by a child asking his parents if he could get french fries instead of a real meal. The mother just stared at him as though he ought to know better and he dropped his head to look deeper into the menu, kicking his feet over the edge of his chair. "What do you think about that?"

"What, french fries for a meal?"

"No—kids. Do you ever think about having kids, like through adoption or something?"

"Not much yet. I've got a lot of years—" I knocked on the wood table— "ahead of me."

Matt closed his menu and dropped his chin into the palm of his hand, looking thoughtfully over my right shoulder. "I'm pretty sure I'm going to want a couple." He talked about children the way most people our age did, like they were something collectible.

I closed my menu, too, and asked him, as gently as I could, "Why didn't you and Allison ever have kids?"

He blushed a little. "Too many disagreements, actually—we couldn't agree how to raise them, like in terms of kinds of schools, and religion. I mean, for example, she was Jewish, and yet didn't want to raise her kids Jewish. She said she didn't see what good it would do them, that they should go their own way, come up with their own beliefs."

"Wait—but you aren't Jewish, are you?"

"No, no I'm not. But that's the point—I wasn't raised with any kind of religion. I was the kid who was allowed to go my own way, and all I ended up was agnostic, without roots. She didn't get it, I don't think, didn't understand what she'd been lucky enough to grow up with. Ask my parents what religion we are and they give you a whole laundry list of sects and denominations in our family, but they can't remember which relative was what."

The waitress came then. She was dressed in yellow, and even had a little white frilly apron. Matt got a club sandwich, and I asked for pancakes.

"And keep 'em coming," I said. The waitress winked at me.

After we finished—I only managed to eat six pancakes, but the waitress patted me on the shoulder anyway—we toured up and down the downtown area. It was mainly one deserted short street, the one we'd driven through as we got into town last night. There was a movie theater there that showed one movie at a time, and seemed to lag a few weeks behind Madison, which generally lagged a couple of weeks behind big cities. Matt also pointed out a pizza place—that and a Taco Bell were the town's "ethnic food" —where some members of the community occasionally met to speak against the Winnebago Tribe's fishing rights campaign. Then there were some craft shops, which we picked around in briefly, winding among the T-shirts with the clichés—*been there, done that*—emblazoned across them, kitschy lacquered wood slices with clocks built in, and arrows, plastic bows, and hatchets.

The highlight of the tour was a candy shop. They were making fresh, wet fudge on marble slabs, spreading it with metal spatulas. The two high-school girls behind the counter were clearly amused at me for being so wide-eyed, finding myself surrounded by sweetness.

"First time in Eagle River?" one of them with that popular, slightly large hair asked. She spoke with confidence, perhaps because she knew I was out of my element and in hers, and maybe a little helpless. I wasn't sure what showed on my face. I was beginning to trust the town, but I was feeling a little off balance, too, maybe because of Matt.

"First time. I'm just seeing all the sights."

"Better drive slow, or you might miss 'em all," she said.

I left with a quarter pound of this, a quarter pound of that, a pound in all, and a thin weekly newspaper, covering the entire county, that I picked up from the counter. Matt called it "the local puppy potty trainer." He had been following me more than accompanying me around the downtown, studying me again, to see what I'd make out of everything. I felt very watched. Me, I wasn't sure what to make of the place. I was just observing, my hands in my pockets, still wearing my trucker's cap, probably not much blending in.

In the car I opened the paper and realized it was a single sheet, just folded over to give the reader the pleasure of having something to open. A lot of it was advertising, including one huge one for the pizza place with the anti–Indian rights meetings (though it didn't mention the meetings), and some for stores in other towns.

The major story was actually about the weather. There were short quotes from the locals about how thick they figured the ice on the various lakes was and where they thought it could stand up to an ice-fishing hut. Yet despite all the media fascination, nobody had gone crashing through into the lake, nobody had been caught and frozen in a winter storm, no power lines had gone out. It was just cold, maybe a little worse than usual, or so said one old resident who'd been in that town for sixty-three years. The headline read "Cold Enough For You?"

"You're now up-to-date on all the local happenings," Matt noted on the drive home. "Nothing has escaped your attention."

I laughed quietly, and watched the trees roll by beside the car, which jounced a little on the rough roads. We were the only people driving along there, and all the houses were set way back into the woods, at the ends of driveways that curved away out of sight. I wondered why Matt had the radio on, why he wouldn't rather just listen to the silence, right there in the middle of the day.

"The Atlanta paper's all right, isn't it?" he was asking.

"Mm? Yeah, I liked it all right."

"When I was down there—" I kept forgetting to ask him what he'd been doing down there— "I read it from cover to cover and was just absorbed in it. All the news, crime, murders. Things must have been crazy growing up there—especially in your neighborhood."

I turned toward him, watching the tree shadows and bright light whip across his face. "Wait—where do you think I grew up?"

"What? I don't know—I just remembered you saying it wasn't such a great neighborhood. Summerhill or something."

I shook my head. "You must be thinking of some other black man. I grew up just outside Atlanta, in an old suburb." It was jarring, trying to impose that image of muggings and shootings on my background of big green lawns and kids playing soccer in the park.

His face went red, like a burn, but in streaks. His face seemed capable of changing colors like a chameleon—blue under his eyes when he didn't sleep enough, gray on his chin when he didn't shave. "Oh, shit. I'm sorry. I guess I just remembered you saying . . ."

"That's okay," I said, and laid my hand on his shoulder. Mainly, though, I was watching the bright color fade away from his face, leaving him himself again.

When the lights went off that night, Matt kissed me furiously, as though he was starved or apologetic and had waited until now to show it. This was the first time he'd seemed to be interested in sex since we got there. Neither of us had shaved since a couple of days earlier, and I could feel my skin react angrily to the scratching. I could even hear the stubble scraping there under the high ceilings of the bedroom, in the deep silence of the empty house and surrounding snow-deadened woods. After a moment, my hand was on his chest and we settled back just to look at each other. Even though there were no lights on anywhere, inside or out, there were enough stars to give our eyes something to adjust to. He was just beginning to come into focus.

Matt had on the habitual expression he carried around with

him most of the time—eyes as wide as nickels, mouth slightly open, childlike. When he first approached me, in a bar in Madison called Manoevers, he had that expression hidden behind a confident smirk that looked posed even through all the cigarette smoke and the couple of beers I'd had. His fascinated naiveté kept bursting out all night as he learned little things about me. There had been something attractive about that expression, in the way that innocence always seems attractive—at least on TV or across some other distance. This night I was waiting to see if his face would change the way it had the previous night. Then, his eyes had become withdrawn and even a little panicked as our clothes came off, the more he touched me and allowed me to touch him. Now, he seemed to burn with what looked like determination.

"What are you looking at?" he asked.

"You," I said simply. "Just looking."

"I know what you mean," he said, and rubbed a thumb over my cheek. "You're perfect. I want to keep looking at you long enough to memorize you. This is so frustrating, I think. I don't know you inside and out yet. I can never wait, because things like this let you really get inside a person after a while, see the world like they see it."

He kissed me again, still furiously, and I settled back again. "How many people have you brought back to this place?"

"What, like girlfriends? Just Allison. It took a long time, too, before I was ready to have her up here, like not until we were married." He smiled. "I'm more impatient these days, aren't I? I wanted to get you up here right away, and never take my eyes off you, until I had you totally memorized, top to bottom."

"Matt?" I asked. "You said just girlfriends, right? Have you had other boyfriends up here?"

"You're the first man I've been with," he said, in a surprised tone that suggested I should have known this about him.

"What? That's news to me."

"Yeah, it's true. I don't think of myself as gay. Or anyway I don't know if I'm really gay. All I know is it's pretty exciting." His bright eyes scoured my face. "Let's just try it, okay?"

As he smiled, he sighed, and I could smell the wine on him, the same wine he'd been bearing into my lips so fervently and that had furnished his look of determination. It was already going to be part of my memory of him, the cologne smell of alcohol playing around his mouth.

The next morning, while Matt was still sleeping, I dug the car keys out of the pocket of his blue L. L. Bean anorak and drove into town, without any interference from the radio. I wanted to be fed before I saw him again, and was just hoping something was going to be open. I figured some diner somewhere had to cater to the hungry old men who went out ice-fishing bright and early. Though it took me a while to find it, I finally happened on a place ten minutes outside of town that was serving breakfast, even though it wasn't yet seven. I liked the fact that, even that time of the morning, a business was open. The previous night with Matt had made me feel very alien in this town again, all of a sudden. This much, though, was good.

It turned out they had buffets every Sunday. A small collection of people, some in flannels and jeans, and others with slacks and plain shirts buttoned all the way up—probably churchgoers

—were waiting to get at the metal pans warmed by blue flame sterno lamps. I stood in line with them, and the man in front of me turned around to look me over once or twice. I was immediately on guard. I realized I'd left my local-look camouflage at home —I was wearing my black jeans and a sage green rollneck sweater —but I smiled as genuinely as I could and said hello. He nodded and warmed his eyes at me, asking,

"Ya on vacation?"

"I guess I'm that obvious, huh?" I said, hoping he wasn't going to say something offensive. I dug a spoon into the scrambled eggs as he took a poached one from the next pan over, adeptly moving it onto his plate with tongs. It was a pretty nice spread, all in all, even if grease was beading in spots on all the food.

"Not too hard to guess," he said. "I think I woulda recognized ya if ya were from Eagle River. Havin' a good time over here?"

"It's beautiful."

He smiled, and then he shook his head. "Now, that's what everyone says. I guess I been livin' here too long, so I don't see it like you, you know? I haven't even said *mm mmm* to this sausage gravy they make in here," he said, lifting up a ladle full of white, thick gravy with brown bits in it, "and that's the best around. Make sure ya have some before ya go. Leave some room on that plate for it."

I told him I would, and we smiled good-bye.

I sat near the window, one of the only people in the non-smoking section, which was nearly as full of smoke as the other side. Still, I had a good view of the parking lot, which was somehow attractive because of the lumpy snowdrifts and the evergreen trees planted around the perimeter. The food at this place was great, the kind of junk I never let myself eat because it makes me anxious.

I spent quite a bit of time in that diner, going back several times for more eggs and potatoes, and sausage gravy to top it all off—it did taste amazingly good, and I smiled again at the man who'd recommended it when I caught his eye. He nodded, and his wife waved. Even sitting across the room, they were as friendly as though they were hosting me in their own home. It was like they were just sitting at the other end of one of those long dining-room tables, passing each dish down my way so that I could be sure to get a little of each on my plate.

Matt and I were supposed to leave early enough that afternoon to get us home in time for dinner, but I found myself wishing I could spend a little more time in that town by myself. I wasn't sure when I'd ever get to see it again. As I sat by myself, next to the window, I wondered whether anybody ever asked Matt, with his sharp clothes and schoolboy bangs hair, if he, too, was a tourist up there.

He probably wasn't up yet. The night before, we'd—against my weak protests—fooled around some more, and Matt had finally gotten up, once the panic had come back into his eyes. When he'd been gone from bed a while, I got up and padded out over the shag carpet to listen at the bathroom door. I could hear his wet, heaving coughs echo from inside the toilet, and I knew that it was more because of being with me than because of the alcohol.

I was nearly asleep when he climbed back into bed and whispered, "I'm sorry." His breath smelled different then, sour, even though he'd clearly brushed his teeth. "I'm sorry. I tried, I really did. But I admire you for it. I really do." I couldn't think of what to say, and my back was to him, so I just pretended to be asleep. I wasn't sure he'd have wanted me to remember him saying that, anyway.

On the way back, I took that fudge girl's advice and drove slowly, so as not to miss anything. Of course, it had occurred to me that Matt might be worried about me—I'd left him a note, but I didn't recall saying much in it. As it turned out, he was still asleep when I got back, so I just took my place with my journal on the couch and waited for him, as the light poured through the sliding glass doors over my shoulders. I'd resolved that when he got up, as full as I was, I'd just pretend not to have eaten yet, and go get some more breakfast with him. It would be easier than explaining.

Fighting

MY FIRST fight since eighth grade happens the same night I get mugged on the corner of 48th and Osage. That's a long time to go without fighting, and that's how you end up so unpracticed you get mugged by a kid, a teenager—not even carrying a knife or a gun, not even pretending by jamming his fist into his jacket pocket. He only has a tone of voice, sounding so sure he wants my wallet, more sure than I feel about keeping it. What do I know, grad student or not? So I hand it over, watch him run away between the cars, and then I sit down on someone's front stoop, looking up at Sara's old brick apartment building and the dripping of the occasional air conditioner. In the quiet, I can hear him running for quite a while.

Even though I'd paused as I neared her place, I never intended to fully stop. But maybe that's why I let that kid mug me—it gave me a chance to stand still across from her window in the dark. Actually, you can't see her window from the street, since she lives on the other side. So she couldn't have seen me either, dropping my wallet into his open hand. But maybe, I imagine, they know one another—they have something of the same authority, certainty, the same selfishness. Maybe she sent him to get my money, so the two of them could order out for pizza at my expense and make love under her swim team photos.

Beside me on the stoop, where he was sitting when I came up the street not paying attention, he's left a wrinkled brown bag with a bottle in it. The cap is still on, the seal unbroken. It's as though we just traded things—he got my membership card to Blockbuster Video, and I got his malt liquor. Almost a fair exchange, or at least it begins to feel fair as the cap twists under my fingers and the fizz fills my mouth. I feel the kick of it right away.

Like I said, it's been years since I've been in one of those shoving matches with crowded kids circling two lone boys moving in a circle themselves, shoulder on shoulder. An impulsive kid, I usually swung first. Not strong or quick, I seemed a little crazy anyway, the way bookish boys always seem when every once in a while they make fists. But my last fight, in eighth grade, was with this huge bear of a kid named Wayne Barber, and he destroyed me. I'd started it, aggravated by the swarms of kids bumping into each other as they streamed through the school halls, but this kid was made of concrete or something. When he got sick of me punching him, he hit me three times in the cheekbones and temple and I found myself barely balancing against the tall lockers, down on one knee. The kids in the hallway stood alert and still, wondering if I'd died so that maybe they could eat me. I was already seeing funny.

The squirmy vice principal with the facial tics told us we had to grow up, that you never saw adults in an office building settling disputes by rolling around on the carpet between the water cooler and the cubicles. But even though he was right about how adults act, I don't know if I ever came to feel his moral enthusiasm about it. Whatever else it gave me, that maturation also left me to get mugged by a kid with no weapon.

For the next half hour, instead of circling the block where Sara lives, I push further south and west, where the houses fall into indolence and even the stoops are deeply chipped and marked, their continued existence hard-won. Where they made that action movie not too long ago, the one I saw last week. I swagger, like someone who's got so much money in his pockets it makes him walk strangely. I'm looking for that kid, trying to draw him out, though I doubt I could actually recognize him unless he still has on the Panthers jacket that went all the way down his thighs. Meanwhile, I drink and drink and replay the mugging in my mind like an obsessed player after a losing game, the same way I keep replaying my last conversation with Sara, the one she snuck past my guard to catch me flat-footed. Each time I replay it I have an answer for her, a response, something. At the time I had nothing. I also review the mugging, but imagine the kid actually attacking me so I can use something I picked up in the martial arts class I once took, one of those abstract moves—coiling kick, flower hands, push palms. It sounds unreal, like artwork.

So I walk, or try to walk, like I have a fat wallet slapping against my leg. I want to look like someone too school educated to know better than to walk around like that, vulnerable, so that I will be attacked. I fight to keep down that raging noise that wells up when someone's taken something from you. That sound, I remember from childhood, keeps people away, and it's loud now, inside my ears.

Deeper than 54th and Hazel, I stand and open my arms wide in the middle of the street, the mostly drained bottle in my left hand, and the desire to feel someone's flesh soft under my fists gets loose. I spit through my wet lips, "I've got money. Come get me," and I watch the words disappear into the few straggling trees. Looking around me, I feel suddenly foolish—nobody would come up and attack a crazy person. The houses slump and stare at me, and I feel my forward motion slump with them, into the soles of my feet.

Sitting again on a stoop, I take in the glamourless huddled homes. It seems to me that this street was one of the ones that made it into that action film shot in the neighborhood, a foot-chase scene or something. I saw that movie over the weekend, on a day so blue and beautiful I didn't have a hope of escaping it unless I hid in a dark theater or a safe. This was exactly the kind of movie Sara would have hated. I hadn't been to an action flick in maybe a year and a half, the way people in couples give up things they like for each other, and so I wanted to see this one. I wanted to see all these old, beat-up street corners and homes on the screen as though they were something fictional. Sure enough —in one scene, I was sure there was a kid I knew from high school, his face pressed up against the window of a hoagie shop.

Anyway, in the climactic scene, this main character, a cop, was down in the sewers, wading through the slop in chinos, shirt-sleeves rolled up, loose fat tie, and carrying a length of pipe in his right hand. He looked like a guy who would definitely settle what should be played on the office radio by wrestling around on the carpet with his coworker. He'd just taken out a bunch of these Japanese yakuza-style gangsters down there in full wetsuits, and he wore this brand new expression on his face.

He looked a little like a high-school kid skipping away from the basket after sinking his first three-point shot. His eyes were wide with excitement, and he kept almost showing his teeth in a smile as the sewer water crept up in stains along his pant legs. He wanted to find that cruel, angular mafia don, the one with the crisp suits and the attractive and redeemable daughter. He could sense him down there, the way a fist tingles right before it lands.

I stand up. I stalk back east and north with my hands in my pockets, and I don't bump into anybody. Midnight's passed, but not by much. I walk down the middle of the street, expecting to be caught in a pair of headlights and nudged over onto the sidewalk, but it's quiet there too. It comes to me that I haven't seen a soul for a long time.

When I get back to Spruce Street, though, having totally avoided Sara's place on this leg, I find lights, and cars, and even some college students drinking beer out of cans, sitting on porches. I've long since emptied my bottle, and yet I carry it, holding onto it with the grip of drunkenness. As I walk unsteadily east from one street number to the next, the 42 bus steams by, whipping a silty breeze over me. I'm on the sidewalk by then, looking for an open bar, and then I remember an old Irish-style pub just down the street, Murphy's or something, the kind of place haunted by ruddy-faced aging white men, the kind who piss green in the back alley every St. Paddy's day. I leave my bottle on the curb.

You can find this kind of bar anywhere in town—wedged in, skinny like an alley, extending way back along a dark wooden bar top. The few men are mostly older, not the college crowd at all, with their shoulders pulled up and forward to hover protectively over their drinks. The beer all looks the same, weak and failing, flatulence even before ingested. The men watch me for some reason as I bounce in off the doorjamb. Maybe because I look young enough to be one of those snotty U of P undergrads or a neighborhood punk, which is what I feel like right now. I don't know how I look. One slack-faced guy seems to be keeping his eyes on me, like he's too drunk to realign his gaze, or like he's decided something.

I realize I've come in bellicose, having decided that the way you start a fight in this world is through preparation. That mugger kid knows that. He stood up so forcefully from the stoop to block me with his script memorized, maybe pockets full of wallets from people who didn't know their parts well enough to resist. I'd been in school—and life—long enough to have an infinite number of things to tell the mugger, and I didn't believe in any of them as strongly as he believed in what he had to say.

I wonder if that single-minded kid sometimes feels doubtful, maybe just after he wakes up in the morning, before his teeth are brushed. I wish I had grabbed him once he had my wallet and warned him against going into Sara's apartment building, told him to take me with him somewhere else. We'd get some pot and go sit under the bridge by 30th Street, look down over the river from that slope rough with plastic and paper trash. But I had too many things to do and say, where he had only one, and that was the beautiful thing about him.

I think about that cop in the movie, too, in that final scene —he had the mafia boss at his feet, wallowing in the sewage, cowering and seemingly transformed from confident cruelty to wretchedness, yet this angular, evil man was reaching beneath the surface of the slop to recover the knife lost at his feet. But the cop sensed the knife coming, a tingle in his neck where it would cut through him. So with a quick move that looked like flower hands from my martial arts class, he turned the blade on the mafia boss, drove it in between his ribs, and said something dramatic like "that's for your daughter," or "you're flushed," or "don't forget to write." Or maybe what he said, though by now I might be mixing up movie memories and real life, was "I don't love you anymore."

That guy in the bar, about forty years old and wearing an Eagles T-shirt, seems to keep staring at me—though in the dark and through my head I can't make out all of his slack face. I feel I've made him look at me, that I pulled his eyes toward me purely through the power of my will. He looks drunk to me, the kind of drunk that smells through your skin, and somewhere in me I know his eyes are probably just locked, that he has some kind of alcohol myopia, not really trying to say anything to me. Maybe he's me in ten years, still trying to regain that sense of preparedness.

I order the most drinkable beer they offer on tap and immediately remember that I have no wallet, and so no money to pay for it. All I have on me is a light ring of keys. That's when I stand up. As the bartender fills up my glass behind me, I walk over to that man in the Eagles T-shirt. His eyes seem to follow me the whole way, like a painting, as I hold onto the tables and a couple of shoulders for support, feeling a comfortable sense of inevitability.

The only thing missing is my follow-through. I walk solidly up to the man whose skinny face hangs on him, and plant my feet shoulder-width apart. Before he speaks, I tell him I don't love him anymore, and then I whomp him in the side of the head—

just shy of the eye socket—with the square of my tingling right fist. Hard enough to make my arm shake a little.

He topples sideways fast, and his chair clatters to the floor, spilling him out, limbs and surprise at my feet. For the most razor-thin moment, I can't help being impressed with my right arm. I must have put some shoulder into it.

But then I just stand there. The air feels impressed, too, and silent in a way that muffles the Peter Cetera on the jukebox some. Silent, anyway, except the bartender appearing in a space behind me. He wrenches me by my neck through a crowd of scattered chairs and onlookers and tosses me with only his left wrist into Spruce Street.

I don't catch myself at all. I just spin and land full-out on my back and feel all the air in my lungs ripped out at once.

"Now get outta here before I call the cops," he says. He looks meaner in between the light of the bar and the streetlamps, and his left hand is still curled into the shape of my neck. Nobody ever calls the police in this neighborhood, since they'd never come— hating both frat boys and poor people   but I still pick myself up to leave, because this bartender is sure I should.

As though this has only been a pause in some long, restless pacing route, I shamble off south and west again. My whole right side hums, a few different voices basically saying the same thing. More satisfying, in a dull and foggy way, is the thought of the morning, when everything will ache the same, my skull from alcohol, my neck, my arm and knuckles, my overused feet, and my mouth, for shamelessly passing on those dangerous words. Who knows what that man in the bar will do next, to get rid of them?

Social Games

THE NEXT morning Sally and I sneak downstairs from her apartment into the Polecat Tap. This is where she works, tending bar, and so she easily finds some potato skins and eggs, fires up the grill. Even though the windows are clouded with the perpetual January Wisconsin frost, it's warm enough in here for her to be wearing a long pajama top, an apron, and nothing else. I've got the pajama bottoms, but I also slipped my sweater back on, the one I wore last night. Last night on our first date. That thought —*first date*—takes me by surprise; I'd forgotten, somehow.

"This where you get all your food?" I ask, changing the topic in my head.

"I know—I act like this is my pantry. I guess that's what it is," she says, chopping at the scrambling eggs with the side of her spatula, the other hand on her hip. "Hey, do you want some hard cider to drink? It's almost healthy, right? It's named after the stalwart woodchuck, after all."

"Sure," I say, though I hope I won't smell like alcohol when I get to school. I'm not due for my student teaching until third period anyway. "Does your boss know you eat down here when you're off duty?"

"I guess so. She's my landlord, too, and she knows my key ring has both rings on it. Not as though I stuff myself, anyway," she says. "Do I seem to you a *thief*?" She spreads her arms wide, defiant, with the spatula above her catching light. I don't know quite how to look at her. I don't know that face, the way one black, shiny tuft of her hair curls loose under her ear, the arching of her right eyebrow independent of her left.

I laugh. "No, no. Hey now, Sally, look out before you burn those eggs. Are you watching them?"

"If *you* don't watch it I might be the only one about to get a free breakfast around here." The way her language switches up, too—I can't believe how little I know her mind for how fast things are happening.

The bar is quiet, all the dark wood absorbent and deadening, grabbing the sounds in midair and putting heaviness on them.

"I don't really like working here," she admits all of a sudden. "Stupid skunk apron, smiling at all the damn customers like I love everyone."

After a second, I say, "So maybe there's something else you could do? Everybody loves people with English degrees, don't they? Businesses, or something."

She crosses her arms, and they are dark like her face. "Maybe. You know, I might like to be an investigative reporter. Though I don't really like to write. Maybe just the investigation part." I can't tell if she's kidding or not, and she turns back to the eggs.

After a quiet moment, I say, "I'm kind of nervous about going to school today."

She stops chewing. "Why?"

"It's a 'Social Game' day."

She arches a dark eyebrow at me, and I explain, "They started this program in the fall, because they decided that the kids aren't getting enough wisdom about the world in the classroom. So they play these 'Social Games.'" I'm nervous telling her about this, as though it is too personal, and I don't know why.

"Like what?"

"Well, they're always a big secret—I don't know how they get away with skipping permission slips, but they do—and so I have no idea what's going to happen today. But there was one a few months ago where all the kids had to wear blindfolds all day so they could learn to listen to each other better."

"Did it work?"

I shrug. "A lot of my students just ended up falling asleep."

In a few minutes we have scrambled eggs spotted with chives and red peppers, and greasy potatoes. The Woodchuck cider tastes almost like regular juice. She sits on one side of the bar and I sit on the other, like she's working there, I'm a customer, and we've been sitting here so long we've become completely intimate. Yet there's still the bar between us, and that's okay, because I need to get some room back.

By the time I've made it through the harsh cold to Madison's Velma Hamilton Middle School, none of the boys are talking to any of the girls. The girls, on the other hand, are swarming around the boys whenever they can get away with it, poking and prodding. It looks something like a mating dance or plumage display from one animal to the next.

In between periods, once they've cleared out and we both have a chance to rest for a minute, I sit down with Colleen, their history teacher. She's my supervisor in the practicum program, the woman who's training me to educate eighth graders so I can get my certification. She has gorgeously thick gray hair that rolls all the way down her back.

"So what's the game? Some kind of battle of the sexes?"

"Basically. It's somewhat awe inspiring, actually. Did you notice how the boys were all wearing buttons today?"

"I think so, yeah."

"Well, they've been instructed that they aren't to speak to the girls. If a boy says anything to any girl, he has to forfeit his button, and she gets to keep it, and carry it around with her. You see?"

"And she's allowed to do whatever she wants to break him, I guess."

Colleen nods, tiredly. "Apparently. You'll have noticed that some of the boys in that last class were already missing their buttons. In any case, after a young man 'breaks,' as you say, he's done, and can speak to whomsoever he pleases for the rest of the day, while she goes off to collect more buttons." She pauses, and sighs. "My understanding is that the girl with the most buttons at the end of the day wins some sort of prize."

"Wow," I say in disbelief. "When I was in school, I bet it would have been the reverse—boys stealing girls' buttons."

Colleen sighs again. "Progress?"

Sixth period, the class breaks into small groups to discuss their upcoming research projects. The assignment is for groups of two and three to choose an important figure in twentieth-century

American history, someone who's not a politician, and prepare a paper and presentation on the impact of that person on history. Half police officer, half educator, I walk in circles around the room with my hands clasped behind the small of my back.

I also think about the way Sally walks. My last girlfriend, Alex, moved something like a lumberjack, but last night at the crazy neon Jamaican restaurant Sally just flowed up to the bar to ask about tables when we arrived. Everything Sally did through dinner surprised me. Not just the walking, but lots of ordinary things like that—crumpling and unfolding her napkin through-out the evening; the way she tapped her lip with a fork while lis-tening to me; even just the fact of a little gray in her brown eyes.

Even when I was completely focused, I still wasn't totally see-ing her. Neither of us was really 3-D yet, something more like $2^3/4$-D, starting to emerge from flatness into full-blown life. Two, three beers in me by the end of last night and seven months since the last time I believed someone might love me, I needed her to be whole already.

To regain my focus on the classroom, I stop by one pair of girls discussing their research on Betty Friedan.

"How's it going?" I ask, squatting by Denise's chair.

"Ooh!" she exclaims, pointing straight at me. "You have to give me your button."

"Denise, I don't have a button. I'm not in the game."

Her partner, Sheri, calls out to Colleen. "Mrs. Roessler, doesn't Mr. Andrew have to give Denise his button if he said something to her?"

"Just *Andrew*," I say, embarrassed.

"Lord, Sheri," Colleen says, "you know he's not in the game."

Denise and Sheri both laugh. "Sike, we're just playing," Denise says to me. "But it's going great, though. We dug up all kinds of shit this week." The kids curse around me all the time, and I figure it's because they know I'm not for real yet. I look over their collection—photographs, pamphlets from the National Organization for Women, a couple of books from the understocked library downstairs.

"Hey," Sheri says, "who's grading us—you or Mrs. Roessler?"

"She is," I say.

"Okay. Hey, Mr. Andy, your breath smells like apple juice." They look at me as if to say, *and that'll be all.*

"Mm," I say, and stand up.

No doubt that Sally and I had an easy way of talking that caught me off guard, a sudden comfort. It was so easy last night at the Jamaican restaurant, in fact, that I felt like we'd entered into an unspoken pact with one another. Ten minutes after arriving, we were already sticky with sauce from the buffalo wings.

I admitted things. I told her that the reason I'd left the PhD program in psychology is that it didn't make me feel useful enough. "I think the teaching certification is just to soothe my conscience, to feel like I'm doing something worth doing."

"Guilt, then."

"I guess so. It's hard to imagine why else anyone would ever want to return to junior high."

"I actually had a pretty good experience," she said. "It was fun, discovering boys."

With the little movements we made toward one another, I saw that the pact was about leaping without looking, at least until the next day. I played with her silverware and she tapped on my glass. Maybe if it had just been a drive for sex, I could have resisted that, but this was something else—the need to have someone inside you.

Alex and I were friends for about five months beforehand, because she was the type that's slow to warm up. Late weeknights that fall we sat around small, tiled coffeehouse tables, talking about the impending end of college. Evenings were still warm enough that we could occasionally take slow walks off campus, watching the lights go off in family homes as they closed down for the day. I spent so much energy trying to read her and say things just right I don't think I actually enjoyed myself all that much with her before we started dating. I was too busy trying to set things in motion, both inside and outside me.

With Sally, though, it's only been a week since we met at the Polecat Tap, and yet by the end of last night I knew what every part of her smelled like—the inexpensive simple conditioner, the salt from the small of her back, the almost lemony whiff from between her legs. I felt like I was stealing. She had stolen, too, but two thieves together are still thieves. The two of us had been hellbent, no conversation at all once her apartment door had shut.

This morning, just before I left, she said, "So am I calling you or are you calling me?"

"I'll call you," I said, but I can't quite imagine it—I don't even know who *I* was last night.

I tutor one kid after school through the Urban League. All the students in this program are low-income minorities and having trouble in one area of school or another. Mike and I meet in the school cafeteria at the end of eighth period to talk about math and French and history, although usually we stray pretty far from the topic. I'm not sure I'm much of a tutor.

"So how you doing, Mike?"

"A'ight," he says. "Lost my button to Pam Green today." He looks like he would lean back to lounge if his chair wasn't just a bench. There's some midafternoon light coming in foggy through the old windows and the grates in front of them, and a few colorful posters about nutrition around us, but otherwise it's just gray and huge, like cafeterias always are. My mind is all over the place.

"Did you try to keep it?"

"Not from Pam Green," he says, his arms crossed over his oversized FUBU sweatshirt.

"Mm. So what do you think about all that? The social game."

"It's a'ight," he shrugs. "I wish *I* coulda won something."

"No—I mean, do you think you learned anything from it?"

"*Hell*, no. It's just games. Somebody must be crazy with all these games."

"So that stuff doesn't have anything to do with real life? You don't think that people act like that in the real world?"

"*Hell*, no. Girls taking buttons?"

I change the topic, get him started on his math homework. On the surface, it's about retail markups and discounts, but really it's an attempt to get students to understand percentages.

At one point, Mike's attention gives out, like mine always did when I was in the eighth grade, and he asks, "Do you ever use this shit?"

"What, math? Yeah, sometimes. I don't know about calculus, but I use algebra." I always say that, but I'm not sure I actually ever use algebra.

"I heard about calculus," he says skeptically. After a minute or two he asks, "You have a girlfriend yet?" He asks me this regularly, and this time I'm not sure what to answer. I can hardly picture Sally's face just now, the image has me so agitated, and I feel defensive about it.

"I don't know," I say.

"You don't know?"

"No. Well, something's just getting started." I suddenly feel younger than him.

"Huh. Well, you calling her when you get home tonight?"

"I don't know."

He eyes me straight on, and then shakes his head, saying, "Don't even know. Then you best figure that shit out. The bell is tollin' for *your* ass."

I try to look at him sternly. "Back to math, Mike."

"I'm gonna get *all* As and Bs *this* report card," he says.

Even though Sally and I both got dead tired last night, after everything, I couldn't stay asleep very long. I woke up because I wasn't in bed by myself, or because there were elbows where I was used to just wrinkles in the sheets, or because she has flatter, stiffer pillows than I do, and they occasionally nudged me into alertness as I shifted on them. Or because her body is smaller than my tenuous memory of Alex's. There were a dozen things in that bed that rankled loud enough in my head to keep me out of deep sleep the whole time. And when I was all the way awake, for the first time I wondered what I was getting into here, and what she was getting into. Even with all this time I've had to study myself obsessively over the last bunch of months, I still don't know whether it'd be good for Sally to have me in her life.

At one point I got up to use her bathroom, which was a tiny thing that seemed to have once been a closet. For some reason, maybe the remnants of jerk sauce or warm beer, I decided to brush my teeth, there in the humble light coming in through the window from the alley. I spent minutes at it, running the toothbrush over and around my teeth, gently along my gums, into each hidden space. Her bristles were harder than mine, and the toothpaste was more sharply minty, the kind that stings if it's in your mouth too long. But still I kept at it, in my half-asleep fixity of mind, until I really got the feel of it. When I squeezed into the narrow bed again beside her, I felt like I was breathing icy vapors all over her. Sally woke up slightly, kissed me tenderly on my minty lips and licked her own before sinking under again. It took me a long time to fall asleep with that strange taste in my mouth.

I stay at school well into the evening, looking at some student papers, and then walk slowly toward home along Madison's isthmus. I am, I know, avoiding getting home because I said I'd call her tonight, and I haven't decided if I'm going to or not. Plus, she might just decide to call me instead, so I take my time getting anywhere in the cold, in the dark. Despite the bitterness, people are out, here or there. People hanging out in front of bars or smoking in front of coffee shops. I hunch my way past them, my hands jammed in my pockets and my mind whirling with thought.

Off the direct course, I eventually find myself in front of a frostbitten park where Alex and I used to roam and talk. We did a lot of that kind of thing. Looking out over the hard ground, I imagine our feet crunching through the brittle grass.

I step into the park. It makes no sense, I think, to be in this place by myself, but other stuff makes no sense, too—jerk joints, sex, Sally wrapping my scarf around my neck before I left this morning. I don't know what the point is.

Still, I walk a bit further through the park, listening to myself think. Close to Lake Mendota, I sit on a cold bench and watch the stillness of the ice. It seems a million feet thick, though I'd be afraid to walk out on it.

Then, noisily, a couple comes up from behind me and sits two benches over under a tall lamp. They're wearing enormous puffy jackets with hoods—green and yellow for the Packers. I can tell they're teenagers, almost young enough to be my students. I'm staring at them, and I know it, but they can't see me because of their hoods. In fact, I can't see much of them myself—even their faces are mostly obscured.

At first they sit spaced a little apart, but then they move so close together on the bench I bet no heat can escape from between them, and they start to laugh, their voices bright in the cold. I watch, and when they lean in, the edges of their hoods seal to one another, until they are just one puffy coat. Their heavy arms grip at one another powerfully. Sitting so still, I'm starting to freeze a little, but they seem okay. When they pull apart, one says to the other, "That's nice." Nothing else.

I can still see them and the frozen lake once I've reached the pay phone at the edge of the park. Now they're facing the frozen surface, still as close as possible, seemingly unwilling to move.

Sally answers the phone after a few rings. It's hearing her that finally hits me, and the fact that I'm relieved to hear her, for whatever reason. And even though I'm outside with the traffic and on a lousy pay phone, she recognizes my voice, recognizes it right away.

Pointing Up

MY LITTLE sister never touched a basketball once until she was twelve years old, but by the time she was fifteen, she could slip past me to the hoop more often than not. The length of her hands made her finger rolls soar in a long, aspiring arc that almost always flew unblockable to the hole, leaving me nothing but air to rebound. I considered myself a serious player, too—not the school varsity kind, but one of the wolfen kids tearing up the neighborhood courts.

I don't know what happened to her between twelve and fifteen. I guess because she'd left behind her physically awkward period for the most part and was basically the same height and weight she is today, her body had nothing to do in those years but hone itself. Maybe it eased her mind to do it. Really, nobody knows how she learned basketball that well. But she crafted and calmed herself on the court in Clark Park, her soil-black hair bound up behind her head and the long angles of her face pointing straight up at the backboard.

Everything in her pointed up to the hoop—from her eyes to the lines of her cheekbones, her forearms, the slope of her back as she pulled over the ball. It was maybe the one place in her life where everything in her led in the same direction. People noticed that—and throwing the rock like she did, everybody in my neighborhood wanted to get near her, that was for sure. But nobody could get close enough to steal the ball, or even catch her attention.

My sister didn't play on the school team either. In fact, the kind of school she was at didn't have any teams at all. There was just a bunch of burnt-out half-teachers, half-counselors, who were weary from dealing with the kids that had been referred to them by the regular schools. They were the troubled kids with all their "special" problems, their half-presence, their strangled emotions. It was a wild place, her school, most people not functioning half as well as her. In class she looked like the victim of a serious injustice, sitting in her overalls stock still while the other kids tore around her with their faces not hanging right on them.

One time, when we were playing one-on-one after the day had fallen down, she told me she wanted to die on the basketball court. It was the first thing she had said out loud in days. She used the same raspy whisper she always used, ducking her face down low while she talked.

"You can die, too, on the court, with me, dying on the court, together," she said, and as I stood stunned in front of her she dropped back a step and tossed the ball up. The rock clanged off the backboard into the basket, everything in her still pointing up that way, just as it always had, just as it would every time she touched the court in her life. The way she looked in the streetlight, tall, sure-footed, angled to the sky, I could see a wet chunk of her trying to break free and tear up through the hoop into the trees. It was like one long rope hanging from the net of stars down into her chest, a rope that wasn't pulling hard enough to free her. She could feel how close she was.

Silent myself, all I could do was chase the ball down and toss it back to her, and it traveled in an arc so smooth, so neatly carved from the air, that I felt it might bridge the world between us.

Getting Back onto Solid Foods

ON THE day I was leaving for Oberlin, my housemate Beth gave me a few of the pancakes she'd cooked for her breakfast, and shared the real maple syrup she'd picked up in northern Wisconsin. She still nurtured me by habit, even though it had been more than four months since Natalie had broken up with me. Most other people had grieved with me for about two months and then they had gotten over it.

"When are you leaving?" she asked. Her voice was deeply Wisconsin-accented, which made her sound all the more earnest and sincere.

"Soon—maybe eight-thirty." It was a long trip from Madison to Ohio, and though I could never remember just how long it was, maybe because of the time change in Indiana, I wanted to get an early start.

"Hon, why are you going?"

"I haven't seen Judith in a long time. I think I need to get away," I said.

"But she's going to have a veggie Thanksgiving, isn't she?

Like fake turkey? I'm getting some people together here, and we're going to have the real thing—even the stuffing with walnuts and mushrooms. We're making cranberry sauce."

"I don't mind fake turkey. Besides, you're inviting Natalie, aren't you?" I could handle seeing her during the week, in the department, and even over weekends when all the grad students got together to drink red Wisconsin beer. But I deserved to avoid seeing her on holidays. Nobody owed me anything, but I had the right to seize peace and quiet when I felt I needed it.

"She might be coming. She hasn't said for sure."

"Listen, it doesn't matter. Judith is expecting me and it'll be good for me to get away for a while."

"You know you can call me if you want, right?" Beth said. I knew.

I had spent last Thanksgiving with Natalie's family in Oberlin. They had combined the turkey day with Hanukkah, my first Hanukkah. Instead of mashed potatoes, potato latkes. Instead of saying grace, which my family had never said anyway, I listened quietly while her grandfather led us in a Hebrew prayer. He was an old vaudeville-style comedian and after he was done with the prayer he rolled his eyes and rubbed his stomach and told us he was on a seafood diet. "Whatever I see, I eat," he said. I liked him, with his lopsided, open-mouthed grin and his birdlike face and feathery hair. I liked Natalie's whole huge family. We were spread throughout the living room at different tables, and I was in the kids' corner, with Natalie and her brother Rob and a cousin of hers who talked endlessly about her favorite musicals. She had played the lead in her high school's productions of *Kiss Me, Kate* and *Our Town*, and knew she wanted to spend her life acting on Broadway. Most of her conversation was directed at me, and Natalie squeezed my knee under the table to say, *I owe you one.*

I had never driven the entire trip by myself until this time and, just to shake the tension out of my hands, I had to stop over and over again. I got a second breakfast before facing the confusing turns and connections necessary to avoid driving through downtown Chicago, in a rest stop that was built into a bridge that overlooked the highway. The cars never stopped passing under me, and I wondered if I'd fall asleep to their rhythm, as though they were ocean waves.

For lunch, I stopped in Indiana, a state that had always irritated me. The time change confused me, the scenery was barren and depressing, and I was sick of hearing about Purdue's basketball team. I always wished that I could just skip Indiana. I bought a chicken sandwich with too much mayonnaise pre-spread on it, some fries, and a large Coke. When I sat down with it, I realized that the only reason I'd bought the large was because Natalie had always liked to finish my drinks for me and my small bladder. It occurred to me that I hadn't been on a long car trip since the last time she and I had been to Oberlin together, and that then she drank almost my entire soda. This time I threw most of it away.

The tricky part of driving through Ohio is that when you get to the near border you think you're almost done with the trip, just because it's the last state. But it ends up taking forever, even at ten miles over the speed limit. Passing the sign for Toledo, I remembered the last time we were there, when I said, "We've come too far," pointing at *Toledo*. "We're already in Spain."

She laughed and sighed, shaking her head. "You make that joke every trip." Her eyes were green and they caught the light well.

"I've made that joke before?" I asked.

"Are you serious?" she looked at me, even though she was usually too tense a driver to ever take her eyes off the road, even for a second. "You make that joke *every single trip*."

"Really? Wow. Is it still funny?"

She conceded that it was.

I turned up the music as I drove past the sign, some country station. If you drive long distances, you have to learn to like country music. I was trying to learn.

I was glad to get in before dark because Judith's house was off campus and I was beginning to forget the layout of the town, even though it had only been a year and a half since I had graduated. I had been back since then, a few times, just because Natalie's parents lived there, and because it was a quiet, soothing town where I had once buried a small but important part of my heart, territory that I had marked. Somehow on this trip I felt like I was creeping into the lion's den with raw antelope steaks tied to my clothes.

In the center of town, I drove around Tappan Square twice, watching the students cross in their fall jackets from one corner to the other, from campus to town and from town to campus. Many of the men had long hair, like I did, and it made me feel incredibly nostalgic, as though I ought to jump out of my car and fall into line behind a couple of students, just blend in. I could go drink coffee at the Fève, where all the employees were hired for the severity of their contempt. It was hard to believe such a New York kind of café could survive in small-town Ohio, but there were a lot of New Yorkers in that town. There always are, everywhere.

Judith lived in the southwestern part of Oberlin, among a lot of faculty houses. There was breathing space between the properties, huge, swelling trees that were mostly orange and red by that time, porch swings. It was the part of Oberlin that most students tended to ignore—the part that produced families, the part that didn't affect them directly. Her house was on Cedar Street, huge and blue. Like she'd told me, there were about six bikes on the lawn. According to Judith, four of them had been there for years and I recognized them because they were rusted into immobility. By the time she'd moved in, they were already lawn ornaments. I weaved through them to the doorbell.

Since the last time I saw her, Judith had dyed her hair blond, but it was still only about a half-inch long. At one time, her hair had been enormous, spilling down and around her tiny shoulders, fiercely red. She was beautiful both ways, though differently. She looked at me sideways with a coy smile and flung her arms wide. When I hugged her I felt and remembered how small she was.

"Peter!" she cried. She had a big voice, bigger than her lungs. "Happy Thanksgiving," she added, though it was a day early. Her cat, Puppy, appeared from inside the house and hovered over the threshold with some interest in me. He was orange, in that brown way that cats are orange.

"You too. You look great."

"My parents don't think so." She shrugged. "But it's sweet of you to say so."

We went out to dinner because it was my first night back, a pizza place owned by a student called Aunt Tina's, where the cooking varied immensely according to who was working on the given night. The night I got into town, they must have run out of cooks completely and been forced to recruit amateurs directly from the street. I eyed Judith's cheese stromboli jealously, which smelled round with garlic and maybe cayenne. But my pesto pizza smelled good, too, and yet tasted like dish soap. I was glad she was paying for it.

"How's music?" I asked. She was a violinist, had been playing since she was three years old when her mother had forced her to begin learning Suzuki on a miniature instrument.

She shrugged. "Things have gotten better. I think I'm back in love with the old wooden box." She had come to hate it for a while, thought instead she might like to leave school altogether. She said she wanted to sell flowers in airports, though it was un-likely that she would have had the patience for it. She went on, "I'm going to go to Spain again in January. Maybe to Italy, too."

I smiled. "Some life."

"If you like traveling."

"Which you do."

"Yes," she said.

There were two other people in the restaurant, a couple of students. The woman's hair was knotted and tangled and she was talking to the guy with her about how turkeys were treated on factory farms. He sneered with disgust.

Judith was talking. "I mean, how are you?" she was asking.

"I don't know. You'd think I'd be fine after four months, right?"

She frowned. "I'd think you'd still feel pretty shitty or else you were never in love at all. I mean, Christ."

"Well, then, I'm shitty." I was trying to decide, while I was speaking, whether I should give up on my pizza and just buy myself some fries or something, or something prepackaged that the cook hadn't touched. I didn't want Judith to feel obligated to pay for it.

"What's it like between the two of you? Are you civil?" she asked.

"Oh, yeah. I gave up the silent treatment a while ago. I couldn't sustain the anger I needed to really snub her forever. So now we just coexist. But I still hate her a little, so sometimes when she says hello I'll just sort of keep on doing what I'm doing like I didn't hear her. Childish."

Shrug. "So? I think she was childish to give you up. After all, she was the one who said she needed independence, right? Freedom, in other words."

"Yeah, I guess so."

"Well, you're giving her independence and freedom. She doesn't have to care about anybody else or take anyone else into consideration, which is what she wanted. But at the same time nobody has to care about *her* or be decent to *her* either, which maybe she didn't want, but . . . them's the breaks. It's a package deal."

"So you're saying be shitty?"

"If it helps you," she agreed, picking at her food. "By the way, do you want any of my stromboli? It smelled good while he was cooking it, but it tastes like a salt lick."

Judith and I stayed up late, talking, and then I slept in her double bed with her, her cat Puppy curled up against my skin. I liked him because he was strange—he slept with his nose buried deep in between the soles of my feet. Right before we went to bed, Judith had pulled out her violin and played me a small portion of an un-

sentimental Bartók piece that she was working on for a perform-
ance. She stood on the tips of her toes and shifted weight from
one foot to the other as she played. After that she fell deeply
asleep, almost instantly.

I enjoyed both her presence and Puppy's. I had been sleeping alone for all those months and I was sick of it. I missed the
insistent press of warmth that the cat was giving me and I missed
the opportunity that Judith was giving me to roll over and wake
someone up to talk, though in fact she was generally pretty tough
to wake. She and I had slept together a few times in college, sometimes with sex and sometimes completely without. Supposedly it
had always been without obligations and consequences, like water
off a duck's back, though I was never sure if it really worked that
way.

When I woke up she was dressing and said she had to go
practice. She was pulling on a pair of life-threateningly tight jeans
over what I thought were green underpants, though the light was
low. I fell back asleep so I didn't have to decide what to do next.

When I finally got out of bed I left to explore Oberlin, though
I had seen it a million times already. I just wanted to be moving.

Crossing the line between off campus and campus made me
feel like a trailblazer emerging from the bush to find one of the
cities of gold. Those cool, lush, residential streets seemed to
sweep closed behind me like full-branched foliage into a quiet
wall. In front of me there was the bony white conservatory with
tiny prison-style windows, variegated dormitories, and stoplights.
Those same stoplights blinked at night, and long minutes went
by between the passing of one car and the passing of the next.
When I went to college there, on nights when I was drunk, I
would sometimes stand in the center of the crossroads just be-

cause it felt somehow impossible to stop in the middle of the street, like standing still on the air just over the edge of a cliff.

I had breakfast in the Campus Restaurant, a place with completely unpredictable hours and waitresses who dressed in banana-skin yellow outfits. Nothing happened quickly in the Campus Restaurant, but I wasn't even remotely pressed for time. I even enjoyed reading the familiar menu, which was still riddled with unbelievable misspellings, my favorite being the chicken-fried steak that came with "mach potatousse."

The waitress was a student, fake-black hair clipped back, and incredibly tall. The fact that she was pear-shaped added to her height in my mind, because the relative smallness of her shoulders and head made them seem farther away. Feeling little in my booth, I ordered what I always used to: the number one breakfast plate, which came with fried eggs, toast, bacon, and potatoes—the sliced kind that never satisfied me as much as the grated kind—plus a breakfast croissant with a sheet of eggs and plasticky cheese and bacon, and one cookies and cream malted, extra thick. I liked the spoon to stand straight up in the drink. Before it arrived, I looked through the little personal jukebox stuck to the wall by my table at all the old New Kids on the Block and Paula Abdul and I watched the other people in the place.

I was on the nonsmoking side. There were a few other tables filled up, people generally in couples. It occurred to me at some point after Natalie broke things off that people tend to move around in twos, out of all the possible numbers in the world. It's the kind of thing you don't notice while you're in a relationship, just like you don't notice that some of your friends are alone and maybe even envious, the way you don't notice that things always have the potential to change. But there seems to exist a massive compulsion for twos. When you're with someone it seems natural, and when you're alone it seems cruel.

I stared at one couple for a while. They were both wearing wool hats, the ones with the earflaps and all the bright Guatemalan colors and the one inexplicable string dangling off the top. From underneath those hats, thick black hair crawled all over their necks and shoulders. They looked woolen themselves. He was trying to explain the term "hegemony" in the context of environmental racism, and she was stealing all of the coleslaw and french fries from his plate with a long, flashing fork. When he finally protested, she tried to feed him a fry with her fork and apparently almost punctured his throat from the inside.

It was too cold to stay outside for long, plus all my warmth was circling around my full, fitful stomach, so I could feel my extremities protesting. But I wanted desperately to be outside because it had been so long since I had last stood on such complete flatness. You could see farther, and I had the idea that I might be able to see far enough to find a very distant calm, maybe even in myself. The crisp air helped.

I sat on one of the benches that, for some reason, faced away from the square and looked instead at the college bookstore. The light was absolutely yellow inside, as though lit by candles. Because it was only across the street and the windows were so big, I could see the cashier standing idly by the counter, looking as though he were trapped on a deserted island just in sight of civilization. I wanted to go tell him he could leave if he wanted to, but instead I just looked. The street looked the same, the suit store I'd never been in except to price belts once, the Chinese restaurant that never gave you seconds on white rice, the old family-owned market where, in the summer, Natalie and I got nonfat frozen yogurt if the flavors were good that day.

I spent my last two college summers in the town of Oberlin, working in the dining hall for all the basketball and cheerleader campers that rolled through when school wasn't in session. The ones I hated the most were the tennis campers, because they treated us like the servants that lived in their parents' houses. It was debilitating, almost, bearing up under the scorn of a bunch of eleven–year-olds. After work I'd search Natalie out and put my head in her lap and let her play with my hair. She liked it because it was curly.

"Just think," she said. "When you're a college professor, they'll be just out of high school. You'll be in charge of giving them grades."

"Revenge, huh?"

"Not necessarily. Just power."

Power, of course, had always been our problem. But the summer in Oberlin was so mild and so quiet you could almost hear blades of grass nestling up against one another as they grew and everything seemed fine.

I looked in the bookstore again. The cashier was working, selling something to a woman with short, dark hair. She looked a little like Natalie's mother, Evy, who had always liked me. Once, when I'd had a week of gnawing doubts at grad school, she'd sent me a box full of chocolate-chip cookies. By the time they got to me, they were broken into a million pieces, but I was still overwhelmed with gratitude. I ate them slowly but steadily, one piece at a time.

When the door to the bookstore opened, letting out a little of that yellow into the harsher white light of the outdoors, I looked closer and realized that the woman actually was Natalie's mother. She saw me at the same time. Some moments you might give up your right arm to avoid. Like that moment when you're about to fall down the stairs and you so tangibly feel that sock foot lose its grip and you see the world, in slow motion, twist, just before you painfully hit that first step with your ass. That's how I felt watching Evy cross the street, and I could see that was how she felt, too.

"Hi," I said, smiling. I hadn't seen her in a long time. The last time I saw her I was sitting next to Natalie in the car, driving away from their house on the way back to Madison. I remembered wishing that Natalie's parents were my parents, and thinking that someday they might be. At the time I still had some of Evy's french toast in my stomach. "How are you, Evy?" I stood, but didn't know why.

"Come here," she said, and gave me a long, tight hug. When she pulled away she held my face in her gloved hands and stared into me with the sharpest blue eyes in the world. Natalie's were more green, like seawater, like her father's. "What are you doing sitting out in the cold?"

I shrugged, comfortable and uncomfortable. "I just want to look at Oberlin a little. It's not that cold."

She stared at me sideways like a mom watching her child getting frostbite because he wasn't properly dressed like she'd told him to be, and then she smiled and sat down. I sat down, too.

"So what brings you to Oberlin?" she asked brightly, arranging her bags in her lap.

"Thanksgiving," I said. "I'm having Thanksgiving dinner with an old friend. A student here."

"Oh—I didn't know you had any friends left here."

I looked down as she said that, shocked.

"Oh, dear, that's not what I meant," she said. "I just meant that I thought all your classmates had graduated already. Not that you've lost all your old friends here."

"Right."

We both looked out over the bookstore. I was trying to think of something to say.

"Well, I wish you didn't already have plans. We'd invite you over for turkey at our place."

I had eaten with them a couple of times without Natalie in the past, because I had achieved that level of comfort with them where I could do that, or leave my socks on the bathroom floor by accident or admit when I was hung over. But never since the relationship had ended. It might have felt like a wake.

"Are you having the whole family over?"

"Amazingly enough, no. It'll just be the old folks, and Rob and Karen." She liked to call her husband and herself the old folks. Rob and Karen were Natalie's brother and sister. I had helped Rob decide on a college the previous year. "We're just having a small Thanksgiving dinner this year. But I've been cooking all the old standards, including the cranberries fresh from the can." She laughed and shook her head. "It would be wonderful if you could come."

"Yeah, it would," I said, and looked down. I was going to cry, something I hadn't done for a couple of months. Evy noticed and put her arm around me, like a football buddy. There was something efficient, clean, about it, as though she was distancing herself from the event. So I cried, and otherwise we sat in silence. There are some silences, it occurred to me, that you aren't allowed to break into with bits of truth and understanding. Instead the leaves picked up and stirred around us, rubbernecking.

When I finally got back to Judith's place she was smoking and making mashed potatoes. I felt an enormously cumbersome overcoat of sadness over my shoulders, wished I could take it off and hang it by the door. I wanted to hide it behind her red velvety winter coat, the one with the white fake-fur collar and the broad pockets. Instead I just hung up my much lighter jacket and walked into the smell of tobacco and something baking.

"What's cooking?" I asked.

Before answering me, mashing potatoes, she swung her little behind and sang, "Hey, good lookin', Whatcha got cookin', How's about cookin' something up with me?". . ." I sat at the kitchen table on an unstable wooden chair painted fingernail-polish red. "Well, you can see what we've got for starch," she said, tilting up the bowl to show me the glutinous mass inside. She had mashed the skins in, too, which is how I liked them. "And I'm going to make green beans, which is pretty traditional, I think. Green beans with almonds, that's what I'm making. You can help with that."

"What about the main course?" I asked.

"We're not having any. Just *les haricots verts* and *les* . . . what's potatoes, in French? *Pommes* something?"

"I don't know. So we're just having beans and potatoes?"

"No, I'm just kidding. I flubbed the joke, though, because of my French. We're having this nutloaf recipe I got from my aunt. You put béchamel sauce on it. Nuts and mushrooms and cheese, but all ground up, and made into a loaf. With sauce."

"Hm," I said, and stared at the table, wondering if I liked things like nutloaves.

"Are you okay?" she asked.

"Not really. I ran into Natalie's mom downtown."

Judith put the bowl aside. "Shit. Did you get into a screaming match?"

I shook my head. "Nah. It wasn't like that at all. After all, she was one of the people who thought Natalie and I would get married someday."

"Really?"

"Yeah. There was this one time that she gave Natalie and me this article on how people from Oberlin always seem to marry other people from Oberlin. How this school has the highest rate of inbreeding in the country."

"God, I know. Terrifying."

"But so she and I were always tight. It was just incredibly strange to see her, because I didn't know who she was and she didn't know who I was. At one point she was my future mother-in-law and now she's just Evy. Just this woman."

"So you talked? What the hell did you find to talk about?" She dragged all the last life out of her cigarette, squinting one eye, and then crushed it in the ashtray on the kitchen counter.

I shrugged. "Not much. I couldn't tell her how much I hate her daughter, or how much I love her daughter, or whatever, and she couldn't tell me whether she misses me or thinks her daughter's crazy or not. When you can't talk about those things, you can hardly talk about anything at all."

Judith nodded somberly. "Sucks," she said.

"When we finally gave it up, she gave me a hug, and when she pulled away I think she was crying some."

"How about you? Do you want a shoulder?" She came over to me and laid her hand gently on my back.

I was exhausted, and my eyes hurt. "No, I already did that. All I want is Thanksgiving dinner."

"You can help with the green beans," she said. "And maybe the loaf. I've never made it before."

I'd called Beth before coming back to Judith's house. I didn't know what I expected, but it was hard, having her distant voice travel into this place that was part of my past. She, and my other friends from school, had been separate from Oberlin, if not from Natalie, up to that point. Now I could hear her as I stood leashed to the pay phone outside Warner recital hall in the conservatory. There was an appliance running in her background, and behind me I could hear brass instruments somewhere nearby. Mostly I was alone, though. It was Thanksgiving, after all.

"Are they coming over soon?" I asked.

"Some people are already here," she said, "helping. How are you doing?"

I smiled, and because it turned out the wrong way around I couldn't manage to say anything.

"I'm sorry," she said. The sounds of the appliances faded and I knew she had stretched the cord into our hallway, where she hung all of her hats. I pictured them: baseball caps, berets, even a cowboy hat, and it calmed me.

"Tell me again what you're having for dinner," I said.

We had dinner a few hours later, Judith, me, her housemates Eric and Kathy, and Keir, the guy she was occasionally sleeping with. He had blond dreadlocks that looked fake, like extensions or something. He was nervous around Judith, carried all the dishes quickly into the dining room when she asked, and kept clapping his hands together, waiting for something to do. None of us looked like we were celebrating Thanksgiving. I was used to my father in a brown turtleneck, or my sister in a rusty sweater, all of us glowing warm and soberly attired, surrounding a neat table with a cloth over it. In Judith's house, none of the chairs matched, and we were all in sweats and jeans, shirts spattered with butter or dried potato, and someone had once carved into her table the inscription *Here I sit*, in front of my place. This holiday was one of the many days, since Natalie had decided she didn't love me anymore, that had felt completely new to me. I was constantly experiencing life as though for the first time, with more fear than awe.

As the dinner began, Judith requested that everyone say something aloud.

"Not giving thanks, necessarily, or grace, or wishes. Just whatever. But I'm going to spend my turn on thanks, just to be traditional for a change. Thanks, everybody, for making it. Especially Peter, who had to travel. Thanks to Aunt Mary for the nutloaf recipe, thanks to malt and hops for the cheap beer before us." She raised her can, opened it, and drank.

Her companion, Keir, thanked her for inviting him.

Eric decided to tell us about his day, which he had spent jumping into piles of leaves with his friends, how he was overjoyed to remember the prickly feeling of dry leaf edges poking through clothing. There were still bits and pieces of brown stuck to his sweatshirt, here and there, and a couple of bigger pieces in his hair.

Kathy told us that her parents had called her earlier that evening, and had filled her in on the football highlights. She missed watching the game with them, even if her father always got too drunk every year. She wished that somebody in the house liked football.

"I watch it sometimes," I said, "though we never did on Thanksgiving, in my house. I don't know what we really did, besides eat. Man, if this was New Year's I might make some resolutions."

"Do whatever you want, sweetie. It's New Year's," Judith said.

"Well, then. Dammit, this is going to be a better year. I'm going to do everything right." My voice seemed to echo in the dining room, as though I was in a bad movie. I wondered if the echo was actually in my skull.

"Fair enough. Let's eat," Judith said.

Everybody began grabbing and passing food. That, at least, was familiar. That was what I was after, the minuscule patterns that had been born before I had ever met Natalie, habits I had formed earlier than the habit of waking up with her. It was like trying to reassure myself with pictures from my high-school yearbook. All I wanted was one warm handhold to make me feel solid, grounded. When the nutloaf, overturned onto a plastic plate and looking like a meatloaf, came around, Judith offered to cut me a piece.

"I'll take a drumstick," I said, and when she got the chance, she smiled and squeezed my knee under the table.

Rebbetzin

"ARE YOU going to be all right?" Nina asked, touching the front of my coat, as though testing for something. We were in the Northern Liberties section of Philadelphia, in front of a bar called Joyce's, after James Joyce. It looked like a broad and uncertain house, with small windows and a small porch and porch roof. From inside I could hear the large noise of people. Outside it was very dark and very cold.

"Sure," I said. It was like a mother dropping her child off at a first day of school. My wife touched my coat front again, testing. And I was nervous, and unsure if I would be all right, but I also felt very bad about that. "We should go inside," I said. "You're supposed to be in there already."

Her face seemed airbrushed in her own visible breath. As usual her dark hair was back in a bun that seemed ready to explode loose at the slightest excuse; there were tufts and strands poking out in every direction, and some hair hadn't made it into the bun at all. Nina looked like herself. "Okay," she said. "Thanks."

I hated that she had to thank me. "I want to be here," I said. And she nodded, and we went inside.

It was the night of Jerry's memorial service. He had always insisted that it be held in this bar, apparently, and had left it in his will that the night was to be arranged by Nina. *Nina will be my rabbi, and everyone will mourn me in an Irish bar,* he had written. *There will be a great deal of drinking and other disreputable behavior.* We had traveled from Vermont to Philly so that Nina could make all this happen.

My wife, like me, was Jewish, but not a rabbi. She was, in fact, an artist. And she had been one of Jerry's art students. His favorite, apparently. And even though she had never done anything exactly like this before, Nina was used to organizing, used to being at the center of unfamiliar people and making them familiar—with her and with one another. She had arranged anniversaries, birthday parties, even conferences, often populated by crowds in which I didn't recognize a face. Events I went to despite myself. In the town where we live in Vermont she had set up several open-door art parties, where people would come into our home and read poetry or show a painting or sing, or maybe even just move in a meaningful way. Events that had always left me scared and feeling cut off from everyone, including myself.

Inside, in a very small front room, the light was yellow and thick with smoke and people, and the sound was the sound of the same conversation happening in dozens of mouths all at once. The sound of comfortable exchange. There were people everywhere, jammed to within a couple of feet of the front door and the cold air we'd let in from outside. A couple of heads turned our way, maybe irritated with that cold air. Nina didn't seem to recognize them, and in fact picked herself up on her toes—still leaving her much shorter than most of the people around us—to try and see where we were supposed to be. And then through a gap she spotted it and pointed. A sign next to the stairs, arrow aimed up. *For Jerry*, it read. She wove her way through the crowd with deliberate moves and I followed behind. The staircase was, after the first couple of steps, clear.

At the top was an older man that I'd never met before. *It's starting*, I thought.

"You're Nina," he said, extending his hand to her as she reached the landing. I was on the step below. "I'm Jerry's brother." Something about saying that made him pull up a little, as though shocked by an unexpected burst of emotion. He shook his head slightly. "Thank you for coming a little early. It shouldn't take too long to talk about things," he said.

"Of course," Nina said. I could feel my heart already. It was hard for me to know what to say or do when I was on the side of things. I had only met Jerry a couple of times, once at a long weekend at our house and before that over dinner and a lot of alcohol. She held her hand down toward me. "This is my husband, Daniel."

I shook hands with Jerry's brother, said, "I'm sorry," and felt like a fool. Every word seems like the wrong kind of word sometimes. He nodded at me, his lips tight, and then walked us through the door in front of us.

"I'll just gather up his wife and the other people involved in this, okay?" he said, leaving us by the door. The room, bigger than the one downstairs, but still the size of a living room in someone's home, was sparsely populated so far, people in dark but not entirely formal clothes standing in twos and threes along the wall. Above the more-distant sound of the downstairs voices I heard a little music in this space, something like jazz, with piano.

Nina leaned in to me. "So you'll be okay on your own?" she said. "I'll arrange things with Jerry's brother and the other people, and then I'll be up front pretty much the whole time, on that stage there, I guess." She pointed to a place where bands probably usually played. I nodded. "Why don't you get yourself a soda?" she said. There was a bar in the corner. I nodded again.

"Okay," I said, and then Jerry's brother was beckoning to her from across the room. He was in a small clump of people. I recognized Jerry's wife. Nina gave my hand a squeeze and then she pulled away, sad, but still looking back at me to make sure about me. I really wished I could be different. My therapist says that being self-aware about these things is the first step.

The people in the room all had beer or mixed drinks, and I thought Nina would say, *That's what Jerry would have wanted.* When he and his wife stayed in our house outside Barre, he'd had his first drink each day at daybreak, when he went outside to watch the sun come up over the hills and fill up the Burlington Valley. I watched him do this once, his head thrown toward the sky and his arms out wide, a glass in one hand. He might not touch anything else until lunchtime, or maybe it would be sooner, but he always started at dawn, and by the time he turned in to bed he would have had a lot more.

But I was trying not to drink alcohol myself, just to see if I could get by without it. Especially in groups of people. I went to the bar and ordered a soda from a man whose face was very serious. I looked glancingly at his face, but not at his eyes. He seemed to take this as grief, and handed me the soda without saying anything at all. It was an open bar.

"Nina's husband, right?"

I jumped a little and then saw that the person next to me was Meaghan Allison, another one of Jerry's students and a friend of Nina's who I'd met a couple of times. I remembered her name and the fact that her sculptures were conglomerations of mostly metal junk that she found in overgrown lots in West Philadelphia, and the fact that she had had a torrid affair with a woman who had been Jerry's wife—not this one but the previous one.

"Yes, right, Daniel," I said, and I tried to seem like I wasn't completely sure who she was either. "Meaghan, right?"

"Right." She smiled, but at the peak of the smile it fell a little.

"I'm sorry," I said again, feeling like a fool again.

"Yeah. Yeah. Me, too. How are you doing? I guess you're the rebbetzin tonight, huh?"

The rabbi's wife. I blinked. "Right," I said, and smiled. "I guess so." Even after the months in my therapist's bright office in Burlington, I didn't know why each word I said had to seem so hot and bad in my mouth, and why I wanted them back afterwards. Everything felt like too much or too little. "I think she's really moved to be able to do this, tonight, for Jerry."

Meaghan nodded and looked down at her drink and back up at me again. She was wearing dark overalls over a black sweatshirt. "I'd love to hear about some of what you're doing these days, too," she said. "Are you okay?"

"I am," I said, but then a couple that she knew came up to the bar and they hugged her both at once. I looked around, saw that more people were coming in all the time, and looked around some more. Meaghan had started crying and I didn't want to stare at her as she did it, so I kept looking around the room and drinking my soda in small sips until it was just ice cubes against my mouth.

I moved away when I could see that Meaghan was really talking to her two friends. What I wanted was to find someplace to sit—sitting would be easier, somehow—but there were no chairs. So I stood by a wall and examined my hands and crossed and re-crossed my legs, brought my empty drink to my mouth again, trying not to look at the people I didn't know. Everybody was in pairs and groups. Some of them were holding each other, some were laughing. I guessed that it was a mix of Jerry's colleagues at the university and some artists and family.

I tried one of my therapist's tricks, told myself I could think about it like a kind of endurance test; if I decided that I would have to spend exactly ten minutes doing this, standing here and trying to figure out how to behave, I could count off the seconds and then, after exactly ten minutes, it would be done.

I thought about Jerry, his lean frame with a potbelly, his big, wide eyes. I had liked him. When he was at our house he cooked us breakfast, because he never cooked back in Philly. He liked the free-range eggs we had, liked the thick turkey-sausage patties we often ate. He would make a lot of noise cooking, wake us up if we weren't already up, and say, "I feel like a boy of the country, the subject of a pastorale. I'm making a *mess of eggs.*"

We were living in Vermont mostly because of me. I'd gone to school in Philadelphia for a change of pace but it had been too big for me in the end. I needed a place where I could often be mostly alone. Nina was doing okay up north, though—her weaving projects were incorporating some of the local grasses and baling wire and other things she would find in Barre. And in Barre they loved her work, were displaying a few of her more im-pressive rugs in a gallery in town. There was one made up of a blend of grasses and the plastic cords used to bind stacks of newspapers that I thought was especially good. But sometimes she did stand on our deck and look out toward the south and probably what she was thinking was that she wished she could see someone besides me from that deck.

The room began to get a little crowded, and then I was in the way of a few people who were trying to find a spot for themselves, so I ended up hovering back near the opening alongside the bar that the bartender had to use from time to time. I stayed very aware of him so I could move when he needed me to.

Then I saw Nina come back in through a door on the next wall. She was still with the group she'd left with. She waved me over, and I went.

"Hi, honey," she said, and she hugged me with one arm. She'd been crying. She turned to the others there. "This is my husband, Daniel."

"Yes, yes," Jerry's widow said with a watery smile. "I remember you perfectly." Her name was Helen and she wasn't Jewish but she had been fascinated with the idea of Jews living in Vermont. And now she said, "The Jews of Vermont are here." She was a translator of poetry from eastern Europe, and very well known.

"I'm sorry," I said again, and I said it again to each of the other family members and friends that were introduced to me in the next few moments, wincing a little bit each time I spoke. I didn't know whether to hug them or shake their hands, and so sometimes I did one and found I was supposed to be doing the other. When Nina pulled away again and said, "I'll see you soon," I was relieved. I went straight back to the bar as though in desperate need of alcohol but really just looking for a momentary sense of purpose, and I got another soda. I saw that the people around me were drinking quite a lot. One or two were unsteady on their feet, and I wondered when they'd started. Nina had predicted many would start before they even came here. I felt strange holding a soda.

Just then spontaneously a group of several men and one woman, standing together right next to me, broke into a school's fight song—Wisconsin's, it sounded like. I jumped again, when it began, and then when other people started turning to look, and smile—Jerry must have had some connection to the University of Wisconsin, somehow—I was caught in their eyes. I shook my head and tried to back out of the way—I mean, it was a really nice thing, these people singing, and you could see that on the grateful faces of the people around, but somehow I didn't want them to think it was me doing it if it wasn't me doing it. I backed away and bumped into someone before I turned and just walked in another direction.

Of course I could still hear the singing from my new place, and they went through the fight song twice, fists pumping, and then stopped, and everyone around clapped. I had been smiling sort of mechanically and then I clapped mechanically, too. But then I wished it hadn't ended, because now people went back to their conversations and I had to stand there again with my drink not knowing what to do. I saw that I was near the doorway to the stairs and I put down my glass and I went out.

I intended, I think, just to go to the landing, but there were people there, and so I went down the stairs, and with all the people in the main part of the bar I found I wanted to get out of there, too. Before very long, I was outside again, in the cold, and watching my breath come out. I thought to myself that I had to turn back around, to go back in there—and after all, soon would be the part where Nina began talking, which I wanted to see, and which would make me the same as everyone else up there. I would be a watcher, like everyone else, rather than a person on the fringes.

Thinking of the word *fringes* made me think of the tallis, the prayer shawl, that Nina had woven out of phone cables. At each of the four corners she'd frayed the ends of the cords so that the individual wires were ragged and loose in the air, and then she'd put knots in them, just as in a real tallis. I liked that one a lot. She liked to weave blankets of things that were almost unbendable, and baskets out of things that were too fragile to hold anything. She liked to weave things together that were natural enemies. She liked to see what could and couldn't be woven. I liked her work very much. And Jerry had been the one who had encouraged her when nobody was doing art like that. He had said to her, *Fuck everybody. It's not up to them to save us. It's up to you to save us.* And she was probably up there talking about it right at that minute.

I stepped off the curb and into the street so I could look up at the second-story windows. I could see people leaning up against the jambs around the windows, see that people were looking off toward the stage. Somehow I didn't mind being outside of it when I was completely outside of it, unseen. It was like watching TV. I thought about the time Nina and I fought because she said my life was getting so small and because the television was becoming more important to me, and she later on pulled out the cable line that had been installed outdoors, and she cut it into pieces, and she wove the pieces together into something like a square. But it wasn't a rug or a placemat or a cover or anything. It was too awkward, too lumpy; it wouldn't sit flat. She put it down in front of the television, which was now basically fuzz, and when I saw it, she said to me, "This one's symbolic. Do you get it?"

We hardly ever fought. But I knew I was a hard person to deal with in a lot of ways. Even though she apologized for a full week after the cable thing, once she'd calmed down, and even though I'd already accepted her very first apology, and she kept apologizing, I knew she was more right than me in the situation. That was when the therapy started.

It was just a party. I went back inside.

Upstairs she had already started things, like I thought she would have. Individual people were making toasts now. A man at the microphone was in the middle of running through all the bets Jerry had lost to him over the years, and the fact that Jerry still owed him money for a large number of those bets. This was a heavy man in glasses who I thought might be a person I'd heard about named Brian. Then Jerry's nephew, who was maybe thirty years old, came up to the microphone and read a letter he'd written his uncle on the day of his death. "You gave me the chance, believe it or not, to decide I *didn't* want to play music. You didn't need me to be anything in particular." I liked that. It sounded right to me, too. Jerry had not seemed to need anybody to be anything in particular for him. Nina said he was still friendly with his ex-wives.

Many other people spoke, almost all of them people I didn't know, though Meaghan Allison was among them. People talked about the enormity of him, the power of his great wide paintings, the way that he was ideal as a teacher, a person who made the phrase *generosity of spirit* make sense for the first time. There were many people, and it went on for maybe an hour of words—repeated and inarticulate and new and right every time. It was incredible—and of course I thought about what people might say about me if I were dead. And I realized that my memorial service wouldn't be in a bar, and that my father would as be uncomfortable speaking as I would be, and that my mother would be afraid to say anything that might be taken the wrong way, and that both of them would have in some way thought I could have done better than die before they did. And then I realized I was doing what a child would do, wondering what they'd all think when I was dead, and I felt ashamed.

Nina spoke last, and she did tell the story of how Jerry had freed her to do her art, and about how for a time she thought he was an emissary from God or something, and yet how he never smelled good enough for that to be true. And people laughed. Her bun was half intact and half completely loose. I thought she was beautiful and staggering. I thought about how I wanted her to talk about Jerry's visit to our house, wanted to have a doorway into what she was saying, but I knew that was inappropriate, too. Instead she talked about the first time she had a show of her weavings, mostly speaker wire and satin ribbons at that time, and how when he came to the show he had dyed his hair and beard white to appear more distinguished for the evening. He had even brought a gold-handled walking stick. "Tonight," he had said, "I'm out for *high culture*." And as she told this, her hand went to her mouth and she was crying. It felt like I had been given an electric shock—I was frozen and panicked. But crying was a natural thing; she did it, and then she finished talking, and she said she'd miss Jerry, and then she told us to drink whatever we were drinking in one continuous drink, all the way to the bottom of the glass. Everyone did it. I didn't have anything, but I lifted my hand and made pretend I was doing it. I sort of couldn't believe myself as I was pretending, in front of everyone. A person next to me winked at me.

After that, people in the group started singing songs—camp songs. People were like children, like full-throated children. And I stood there and held my hand in the shape of a glass and looked at my shoes. We were back to the part of the party where I didn't know what to say or who to say it to. I could feel my heart again, and was sad to think that I'd heard about such a big and bold human being and that I hadn't managed to learn anything.

I thought about how, just before he left our place, Jerry said to me, "The next time I see you, I'd like to sketch you."

"Really?" I said.

He smiled. "I doubt you'd like the experience very much. I expect it would take hours to really capture you." He reached out and touched my face with his rough hands and held it still, kept me from moving. He hadn't had anything to drink that day, and although he was staring at me and my heart was going fast at first, everything else was steady and calm. Then he let go, and said, "But I would really be grateful if you would let me." And he and his wife left, and I didn't see him again.

Soon Nina found me, and when she did, she said, "Are you okay?" She came right out of the crowd and by the time I recognized that it was her, she was saying that.

"Yes," I said. "It was really nice." I stood there holding my imaginary glass and not saying anything more. My wife looked at me strangely.

"What are you doing?" she said, gently. So gently it was painful.

I didn't answer. I had started to hold my breath. I decided that I was going to hold my breath until I could manage to go a whole second without thinking of myself or my needs in a room of people who had come together to mark the end of a full and powerful life. But it didn't happen, and before I passed out from holding my breath I gave that up too.

Searching the Reef
in the Off-Season

EVERY STORE on the island is a jewelry store. They prom-
ise 75 percent off and send into the street the glow of display
cases and shocking rushes of air-conditioning, like bakeries vent-
ing the smell of cinnamon pastries out among potential customers.
At door after door, people engage us as though in conversation
while actually delivering sales pitches, even though we're clearly
just walking by—*you know, it's a perfect time to treat yourself, and ladies,
once you've checked out our competition you'll see*—and halfway into the
block we are moving at panic speed, just trying to find some kind
of place where we can breathe. We stop at a corner free of hawk-
ers. The air is hot enough to sting.

"It's a little overwhelming," my mother says, a wild look about
her. I look down and stare at her skinny hands, at her naked ring
finger, until I realize I'm doing it, and then I look up at her strange
face. "Don't you think so?" she says. This vacation was her idea.

"Let's go to that upstairs place across from the ferries," I say,
taking her arm gently. She has lost weight—more than she should,
maybe. "Get a tropical drink or something." From the minute I

got home after graduation, there have been these flashes where she's been the daughter, and I've been the mother.

We sit on a terrace overlooking the dense traffic and the water that is at least as blue as they said it would be. It's funny—this is just the kind of place I should have been going to for spring break these past four years, I guess. And now I'm here after college, abducted, almost, because my parents are getting divorced. We're drinking some surprisingly good carbonated grapefruit drinks.

"This isn't what I expected," Mom says, shaking a worried head. I think again how her face is so much sharper than I'm used to and I want to touch my own face to make sure it's still soft. "I sort of thought there would be more . . . I don't know," she says. "This isn't what I expected. And that hotel." She shakes her head. This is difficult for me to handle—my mother isn't the kind to show when she's unhappy, to break cover. Or at least she wasn't, before.

"The fort was good," I say. Walls twenty-one-feet thick. We went there after lunch to escape the endless shops, but then had little choice but to plunge back into them when the fort was exhausted.

"Yes," she says.

"Anyway, we've really done the town. We can stay away from those streets now," I say. "There are other things to do. Maybe it's still early enough to go to that aquarium today."

"I suppose we could," my mother says, brightening a bit.

Coral World is one of the things that keeps getting recommended to us by locals, taxi drivers, hotel owners, waiters, as though everyone is given the same tourism bureau script to read. They say you can snorkel in the bay right there, afterwards. But even though I've heard this line multiple times, and even though I feel responsible for making this all work, I don't actually know what to do with us. We are on a tropical island hundreds of miles from home, trying to escape our lives in favor of something more ideal.

We gather our things, prepare to make our way.

Then, as we reach the street again, the rain starts.

This is the off-season for these islands, technically the very beginning of hurricane season. Prices are lower but not low, streets are more peaceful but not peaceful. And when it starts to rain today it does so with abandon, drops fat and soaking, our open-toed shoes running with water, our clothes still hot but now heavy, too. And all around us the shutters of the shops and restaurants begin to pull closed.

"The aquarium is probably mostly indoors," I say, the two of us huddled under an awning.

"No," my mother says.

"You don't think it is?"

"I mean let's give it up," she says, dripping despite the awning. "This day is ruined. Let's just go back to that *place.*"

The bed-and-breakfast sounded excellent over the phone. It is not. The room is virtually windowless, and the high ceilings only add to the sense of having been dropped into a well. The people running the place are a happily married but kind of batty couple, people who talk and talk about their long marriage and don't seem to register what we say in polite return. This morning, after one soggy supermarket pastry and our hostess's long monologue on grandchildren, my mother was quick to get out of there, start what she was urgently calling "a couple of girlfriends out on the town."

The climb down the considerable hill from the bed-and-breakfast then took more time than we'd planned on, and because we got lost, took us through unexpected neighborhoods, ones with sagging houses, tires littering porches, young men sitting idly in doorframes. I wondered if this was a safe place for two women to be. And then, suddenly, we were in that strange jewelry theme park of a town.

While my mother is in the shared bathroom down the hall, showering for some reason, I sit dripping dry in the cell-like space and use my card to call Dad at his new number. I'm doing a safe-arrival call, a tradition with all of us. I don't know why I didn't call him yesterday, when we first got in, but I didn't. As it rings, I think about what his apartment must look like—I haven't seen it—and I think about what our house looked like when I got back from college, completely surprised to find a half-empty home, completely surprised to find out my father didn't live there any-more. They had sat together through my entire graduation, with unreadable faces.

He isn't home, as I knew he wouldn't be, and I leave a message while picking at the chipping polish on my toenails.

Mom finds me, having made herself refreshed and deter-mined. She has even blown her hair dry, as though we're still going out tonight. Right away my mother offers a brisk smile—she certainly knows I called my father, but we are not going to mention it. Her cover is back on. "Let's play cards," she says.

Rummy 500 is our game. I nearly always win, even when I try to lose on purpose. My mother is always too busy thinking about something else to pay careful attention to what cards have been played and what cards have been picked up. Now she is even more distracted. I discard card after card that she might be able to use but only sometimes does she pick them up, and many end up lost in the pile.

"Tomorrow will be better," my mother says. I am looking at her naked hand again. "Today wasn't so great."

"Well—"

"But tomorrow will be better. I think we can just forget today." Her face looks like it could break if I touched it wrong. "We'll go to Coral World first thing."

"That sounds good," I say, tossing her a king that I know she needs. Still she passes it by, and draws from the facedown deck instead.

That night, sleeping a foot away from my mother in the one double bed, I have a nightmare about tropical fish. All around me, fish of every sharp shining color possible, shaped like shovels and needles and fists and pieces of paper, mouths like beaks, like human lips, like tubes, eyes bulging or flat, all strange and alien.

In the morning we start for the aquarium with little delay, calling a taxi after another soggy insufficient pastry and another monologue, this time about how much the owners of this bed-and-breakfast want to sell the bed-and-breakfast, and how much trouble they're having doing it. People who can afford it don't want to work so hard, and people who want to work hard can't afford the place.

The taxi ride takes us along a seemingly unrepeatable route of curving and unruly roads, roads carved out of the base of the mountain that this island primarily is. Getting out of town is nice

—I see the kinds of things I'd been expecting, like trees covered in bright tongues of flowers, shacks selling tropical fruits, kids at recess around open-air schools. We go by low walls covered in murals, most of them political. One has a stark painting of a body splayed out dead, and over it the line, *This is Blacks-are-History Month*. Something about this is actually heartening; these paintings, at least, are not put here for tourists.

My mother leans forward to address the driver. "Why are there so many jewelry stores in town?" she asks, very brightly.

"Taxes," he says, his island accent just as advertised. His skin is deeply dark, almost able to accurately be called black. "You can bring home all the duty-free things you want. Gold, rum, cigarettes. Whatever."

"Now, do you really *like* all these tourists?" she asks, and I'm immediately embarrassed, despite myself. This place is dependent on people coming and spending vacation money, dependent on us being in this taxi. We speed by a mural of faces of what seem to me to be African leaders, though I recognize only Mandela.

"Of course," he says. "Without them we would not survive." It's hard to tell exactly what he means. My mother, however, is satisfied.

The aquarium is expensive, like everything we've encountered since we got here two nights ago, but we press forward. We are not going to be stopped. The first small building we enter has us surrounded by a continuous tank, fish like scattered wild tropical flowers swimming a circle around us. Their improbable flowing, flapping fins keep them flying at eye level, separated from us by an inch of glass and a wholly different way of existing. They are not scary, as they were in the nightmare, but I feel a painful yearning in my chest as I watch them. I touch the glass, and can feel how thick it is, somehow. My mother busies herself completely with the placards, tells me that she's read this is the largest actual coral reef display in the world. The other aquariums' displays don't use real coral.

In another building, one with many separate little tanks, she tells me that even though coral reefs take up about 1 percent of the ocean floor, they contain a quarter of the oceans' plant and animal life. I study the bizarre seahorses. The placard that says that they mate for life catches me very much off guard. I move on to other tanks, consider the unrevealing eyes and faces of these darting, floating, remote creatures, and keep touching the glass. The angelfish, the spiny lobster, the puddingwife. Coral, my mother tells me, no matter how much it can look like a plant, is always animal, hundreds of them hidden away making these waving structures a half-inch at a time.

We go over to the building with the predator tank, where nurse sharks and tarpin circle us. It's unclear whether they really see us or not. My mother continues to collect and disseminate information—sharks can smell a tiny drop of blood from a mile away, and up close can actually read the electrical field that all creatures give off. At one point, two remoras suction themselves to the glass, as close to us as anything has gotten, but still apart.

Then we go to one of the outdoor pools where, just below the wall, within reaching distance, little tiny sharks cruise the waters. Mom stares hard at them.

"I can't help thinking of your father," she says.

I jerk up from the wall, in shock. "What are you trying to say?"

My mother gapes at me, equally shocked at my tone. "What, honey?"

"Are you going to start bad-mouthing Dad, now?" I say, amazed to be so angry all of a sudden. I am full, completely full, of anger. "I guess you stopped yourself from bad-mouthing each other in front of me for the whole marriage, but it's going to start up now, now that . . ." I am shaking.

"What? Honey? I wasn't—I wasn't going to—your father would just love it here. I was thinking about that. That's all." She is watching me closely, disoriented.

I feel something drain out of me, but not everything. Still shaking a little, I put my elbows back on the stone wall. The sharks continue to circle. Everywhere there are signs telling us not to put our hands in the water. I want to anyway.

In a few minutes we have both tried to put the cover back on, but still it's not right somehow. We are moving gingerly around one another. And I suggest that we do the snorkeling in the nearby bay, partly because I know that my mother will not go into the water, and so I'll get away from her.

And that's what happens. She sits on a bench up on the grassy hill while I change into my bathing suit, and she stays there, watching me, as I go down to the beach and rent equipment from a deeply tanned white man with messy hair. He asks me if I've ever done this before, and I tell him no.

"It doesn't matter," he says, bright teeth emerging. He winks. "Just take it slow."

We test the seal of the mask on my face, try on flippers for size. And then I take it all off again and walk up to the water. It's warm, but not as warm as I expected. I sit in it, getting used to the temperature, and put my gear back on.

The man says, "Just stay close to the rocks. You won't see anything much over the sand—fish like what grows in the rocks, in the coral. It's like desert and forest." And I think about how, according to what my mother read, 99 percent of the ocean floor is desert, and only 1 percent forest. Down here, every beach you go to has forest. That's what they tell you. "One more thing," he says. "Don't touch anything—you could destroy a hundred years' work by these animals with just one brush of your hand across some coral. Might as well leave the fish alone, too, while you're at it." I nod.

On, the mask seems strange and useless, makes it really difficult to see at all. I look all around, trying to catch sight of where Mom is, but can't make anything out

Then I put my face into the water, and everything changes. Suddenly it's underwater where I can see best, breathe best. Through all this clarity, I could count the grains of sand below me. I stay in place, just enjoying my vision. And only after I've dwelled in that feeling a while do I kick out toward the rocks.

There are other people in here with me, other unidentifiable souls searching the reef for whatever it is they want. And also all around are the plantlike coral, hard at work, and the fish again, the same ones I just saw, as though they've broken free of the tanks to join me out here. I float to them, just let them swim around me and pick at the coral, a gently busy world of color and fluid movement. It is gorgeous, incredible, stunning. The other people nearby are hovering just like me, in apparent awe.

Then, in a burst, I'm surrounded. In every inch of space, thousands—hundreds of thousands, maybe—of tiny silver fish, all in a streaming mass on all sides of me. Everywhere I look, there is living light. It's like being caught in an explosion, but safe. It's like being held, but by a glow. And despite what I've been warned against, I reach out. I want to hold this light that's holding me. I want to touch this unthreatening fire. But everywhere I reach I find nothing—the baby fish effortlessly put themselves just far enough away to avoid me, speeding up, slowing down, shifting. And I turn, see that though I'm surrounded, they're at all times keeping their distance. What they are doing, really, is not holding me, but holding a space, a display case, around me. A sharp and clear space in the water that cannot be reached across.

I have floated with them away from the rocks, and just below me I see sand as the tiny fish stream off and away from me. This time it does feel like a desert. And inside me there is something unbearable. It's the idea that comes over me that I have to choose —I can stay down here in this desert, this untouchable world, or I can stand up, call out to my mother and try to tell her what I'm seeing. But there I'll fail, too. With this mask on, as soon as I come out of this space, I won't be able to see at all.

Orange

THE NEXT morning we are still wary of one another. Our bodies will remember it as the first night since she arrived that we avoided touching one another, and what with all the talking before we slept we have nothing to say right now, this her last day here. We sit on opposite ends of the bed, leaning against the close walls that wedge us in. We slept in the same direction, but now we're sitting on opposite coasts.

She breathes in and out, watching me through what seems like humidity, or haze. This is what words do, create a fog that hangs over two people on two ends of a bed.

Then she goes through her travel bag on the mattress beside her, pulls an orange out, and slowly turns it with her active fingers. She plays piano and says that, with my hands, I should play, too. There are all sorts of things one or the other of us should do. Her fingers are nimble, and as they turn the orange, they look like ten individual creatures, each searching. Then, one thumb finds its spot and she digs the nail in, piercing the rind and pushing her thumb under it. She looks up at me, then, almost with shyness, because she is embarrassed to be proud of the way she peels an orange. But I'm impressed by it, too.

She brushes her long, thin, blond hair behind her ears with the other hand, but never takes the one thumb out from under the rind. Then she returns both hands to the orange and begins working at the peel slowly, paring it up off the orange in a long strip with that same thumb. She is fully intent, and so am I, as though she's trying to teach me something. The strip grows, a long corkscrew. She winds her way around the orange carefully, until the peel is hanging on by only a small spot, and then she works that off, too. She's done it in one continuous strip, and again she smiles up at me. Her embarrassed pride over this small thing seems to make our awkwardness over larger things silly, and I smile back.

She asks me if I want any. I pause, and then ask her for the peel, which she hands me, amused. Right away she digs her thumb in again, separating wedges from wedges, while I carefully finger the peel, massaging and shaping it until it looks whole again. If I hold it carefully, it could almost be a whole orange, inside and out. She and I sit quietly, on opposite ends of the bed, not saying anything.

Out in the Open

ON SHABBAT evening, I walk through Old City among young artists who absolutely don't know that my wife is gone. Even my existence is off their radar, I can tell. As they lope along, underfed mostly, clothes extra big to increase the sense of their hanging off the bodies, their darting eyes skip me, center on other clumps of people in their age range, or on the few clearly wealthy people who might be inclined to buy if the galleries were open. In all of this, I'm invisible.

Filbert, a side street running at first along a fenced-up, locked-up park, appears suddenly on my right, and I take it. Filbert is paved with cobblestones. So much of Philadelphia in the low numbers is in cobblestones, and as much as they wreak havoc on automobile suspensions, people here won't stand for having them removed. Tradition has always been the true mayor of this strange city.

There's a little light in the gallery to my left, and I see what could be a copy of Van Gogh's painting of the starry night, and then I walk on, on the stones. There's nobody else here, and just as I begin to wonder about this bar I think I've heard of, a court-yard appears on my right and I see the sign.

Amidst all the stomach rumblings is another strange sensa-tion. I notice it with my hand on the door handle, and look around, back at the courtyard. Unlike the rest of my world, it's not dyed off-color here. It's all whatever color it actually is, the parked cars, the apartment building to one side, the sky itself. And so the sensation must be, and is, happiness. I'm feeling a little bit of that, or something very much like it.

I have never been in this place, but it doesn't matter because it's absolutely the right one. There's nothing upstairs, behind the door—just steps leading down. I want a basement, somewhere to be even more invisible, and I'm going to get a basement.

Then I stand at the foot of the stairs to take it all in—the brick pillars and walls, the crush of the low ceilings against the tall tables and stools, the shadowy lighting, the space not very crowded yet. It's early, of course. People take their time shifting between work and play.

"You can seat yourself," says a young woman into my reverie, a young, blond waitress who's probably in college somewhere. Her hair is in a tight, short ponytail, a defense maybe against the chaos of customer service that will have shaken her by the end of the evening. Or maybe it's that way because college students are so generally tight these days—their straight hair, their gym-made muscles, the treated, taut skin, the clothes that stick to them, their student-as-consumer orientation.

"I'm just looking around," I say.

She was blowing by me as she spoke, but something in my response stops her. "That's okay, too," she says, and she stands beside me with her arms folded, surveying the scene too, order pad tucked away. I feel like I could almost say to her, *Nah, let's go somewhere else,* and she would come with me, pad and all.

"Should I stay here?" I ask.

"What?"

"Do you think I should stay here?"

She shrugs beside me. "Are you hungry? Or they have a lot of kinds of beer, if you like beer."

I am desperately hungry and thirsty right now.

"I'm going to sit over there," I say, pointing to a corner, and she nods soberly, arms still folded. It's our last moment as companions.

"I'll be right with you," she says, releasing her arms and flapping her pad loose.

Mostly empty, this place. I cross the pillared space a little bent over, because the ceilings are low—not low enough to require bending, but still. This dark room should be a Bedouin camp somewhere, it's so secret and promising. I sit where I can take it in, my back leaning against the ridges and crags of brick wall, and pick up my menu, which is the perfect thing, contains the perfect things.

This is abundance. So many kinds of beer, and then all the fried stuff. I think only briefly about how Rebecca never held these indulgences in much regard. She drank, to the extent that anyone else did, maybe less, but she didn't care much what was in the glass, didn't prefer one thing to another, didn't ever have much at one time. And the greasy stuff—*sat fat,* she'd say with big spooky eyes—just meant more to run off her body later. And so this kind of abundance didn't impress her, and maybe it didn't even strike her as abundance. She was always someone who drank when she was thirsty, and ate when she was hungry. I, of course, am both thirsty and hungry, but that's only part of the point, the beginning of it. Maybe because I agree with Rebecca now about all this, I am going to go beyond what my body needs, force it not only to stop complaining—I'm feeling the internal clamor a bit more now, my happiness shifting into something less pretty with time—but to go further than satisfaction, to a point where it might start complaining about excess.

The waitress arrives. I want to know what her name is, but I don't ask. She's standing across the table from me, all pad and pen now. I want to know her name.

"Have you had this?" I stab the name of a Belgian white beer with my finger, turn the menu to face her. She leans in, friendly enough.

"Yeah," she says. "It's really great. It's big, though, right? Twenty-two ounces."

"Drinking for two," I say, pretty much to myself as I haul the menu back in. "I'll take one, and some jalapeno poppers, and . . . what else?" I want to provoke her back to my side.

"I like the spicy fries," she offers, but she frees herself from the suggestion by shrugging.

"Right," I say. "And one of these southwestern veggie burgers. I guess they come with fries anyway." It's a powerful script, the restaurant script. We can only deviate so far, and that's that.

"Spicy ones?" she says, checking my nod. Maybe I imagine it, but she seems to feel the strain of being trapped in these lines, too. She seems to wish things could be different. Immediately I know for sure that I am imagining it.

The time between the ordering and the getting of the beer is too long—not too long to actually account for getting it, or by any restaurant standards, but just for me right now. There's beer at home, my body whines, and I squeeze hard a pinch of flesh at my stomach. There is also food, and a bed, and never mind all the things remembering Rebecca for good and bad and gone. In flashes of those things, I realize how fragile my mood and general mental state are. I'm desperate for the beer, and I squeeze that paunch hard enough to leave a mark.

When I left the empty apartment tonight, I didn't know where I'd end up sleeping. Maybe someplace luxurious is what I was thinking at first—there's a bed-and-breakfast on 2nd Street, near all the historical things, surrounded by a sea of cobblestone. It can't be a busy season for them, I figure. But thinking about this is a reminder of how few people I know in this city. How moving here to be with Rebecca was the same as closing myself up in a room with her, a room that seemed enormous when all was well and when *love* was the kind of word we used as though we'd forgotten a lot of other ones, and yet which by the end seemed small, and that is only tolerable now, I realize, because I'm not in it. I'm not in that apartment. I'm here at some bar with a beer just arriving, bottle like a wine bottle but thicker, heavier glass, and even if I did know people in Center City, I wouldn't be calling them now. I'm *away, out.* And if my stomach misses the refrigerator it spurned at home, I'll teach it things. I never could handle spicy food, especially not with alcohol.

This is my kiddush, then. It's supposed to be the fruit of the vine, not grain at all. But I guess I'm not doing Shabbat.

The place begins to fill up. It seems that each time I raise the glass to drink and then lower it, there are more people. The glass becomes a magic handkerchief that, with a wave, makes young people appear. It strikes me, naively enough, that none of them can be observant Jews, not if they're carrying on in here on the eve of the Sabbath. Even the Reform, the Reconstructionists we knew would be at home now, in some way resting.

My food arrives. The glass is full, the plate is full. I drink from both, put my teeth into both. What I swallow is a volatile mixture of solid and liquid, the sharp bite of spice jumping on and off my tongue, my stomach quickly becoming overwhelmed. I look up only to notice the growing crowd, and that waitress. She looks at me from very far away, and it almost seems like she's upset, maybe at the abusive way I'm taking all this bar fare into my system. I am not now, if I ever was at all, one of the tight people she knows from college. I'm loose. Visibly, painfully loose, and giving myself more slack by the gulp. I look back to my table to allow her to gawk without feeling impolite.

That's the only way I'll spare her feelings. Very soon I call her over to get another one of those wine-bottle beers. She is not a person who would cut someone off, and I'm not drunk anyway. I don't know why, but I'm not—maybe I'm too driven right now, too focused on satisfying and punishing my stomach and everything else. I won't even let my body get up to go to the bathroom.

I lift my head up for breath, feel my face wet—beer or sauce from the burger or sweat—and pant at the crowd, who ignores me. I'm still invisible to almost everyone here.

"Is it okay?" She's back, beside me again, asking not the required question but more. Is it okay, Are you okay, You're not okay—she's after all these things.

"It's a lot," I say.

"Yeah." She kind of sighs, looking with those knit eyebrows and squirming mouth nothing like Rebecca ever did. Rebecca's favorite emotions were never distress or sadness. "Do you want me to take that away?"

I shake my head no. "Another of those beers, I think." This seems to pain her a little, though I'm sure I don't seem drunk. I may well seem miserable, though. She collects my empty bottle, squirms her lips at me—hasn't smiled at me yet, I think—and walks off. When she's too far away to hear me, I ask her, "What's your name?"

The veggie burger has maybe two bites left. It's too much, along with everything else, and I'm not remotely hungry now. But I want to keep it here. Another beer arrives, and I only think to look up after she's left again—I notice her more when I'm asking for something, less when I'm getting it.

Staring at the burger seems to bring my stomach back to life, to complaining life. Why eat this way, my stomach complains? Not used to spice, not used to excess, not even really used to eating at all; there could be trouble later. Or soon, maybe even soon, my stomach threatens. We'll see, I think.

I check my watch, and am immediately stunned. It's still so early! How ferociously have I been eating? I'm disoriented all of a sudden.

I'll drink this last beer slowly on purpose, slow everything down. And I'll use it like a magic handkerchief, not to make people appear from thin air—there are already enough of them—but to make her appear in and among those people, in different places. See if I can follow her, invisibly, while drinking.

Lift, drink, lower.

She's at a nearby table, her pink tongue over her upper lip, writing on her pad. Does she get tired, writing against nothing but air and her palm?

Lift, drink, lower.

Rebecca—yes, now I see Rebecca—gets home and is out of her clothes within a minute, replacing them fast with gray sweats, and then she's out the door again. She won't reappear until sweat has made all her clothes heavy and dark.

Lift, drink, lower.

She's walking toward the bar, weaving through the crowd, parting it with a gentle hand on a shoulder or a back. Things roll off her, I can tell.

Lift, drink, lower.

Another time. Rebecca watching me, silent and miserable, across the gulf in the living room.

Lift, drink with my teeth on the glass, lower.

Mostly obscured, at the bar, lifted up on her toes, leaning on her forearms. Her calves are sharply defined, two turtle shells. I can't help it—she is powerfully attractive.

Lift, drink for a time, breathing through my nose, lower.

She's right in front of me here in this smoky basement, but she's Rebecca, much less tight, sloppy wavy hair, face with two moles, little cute ones, on it, brown eyes that could be all the colors at once, they're so striking. She's wearing that red T-shirt that says Phillies, but in Hebrew letters. She says, *Listening to you I feel like I'm just hearing the other part of me.*

Blink. A bar again.

I'm done here, I guess, even if it is early. Neither of the two hers around, I slide to my feet off my stool, and the tide of alcohol rolls in. It feels like a tide, though faster. I smile, because it feels good to be drunk, even if my head is still rambling on with obsessive verbality. I enjoy it all the way to the bathroom, all the way through the stream of piss that seems neverending but that is full of a continuous sort of reward, and then all the way back to my table.

I get back on my stool—I haven't paid for any of this yet. Yet the alcohol stays with me up here. The room looks wobbly, flooded with water, and I keep smiling.

She appears, fingers at her pad, ready to pull my check free, hoping I'll stop my ferocious orgy. She's beautiful, could be some prom queen from Wisconsin if she was a little heavier. "All set?" she says.

"Never," I say. "No, yes. I am." I can't stop smiling, which seems to embarrass her.

"Okay." She rips out the check, turquoise with lines, yellow copy left for her. "Thanks."

I look at the paper instead of her. It, too, says "Thanks"—no exclamation point, a serious woman—and also her name, but I cover that with my thumb before I can decipher it. I don't think I can safely know her name. When she's gone, I just apply the right number of bills and stand up again. There's a little burger left, a little beer.

Lift, drink the rest, lower.

She's back at the bar, reminding me of sex again, through no fault of her own.

I grab the veggie burger and stuff the last two bites into my mouth, and swim to the steps, chewing.

The whole city is filled with water, cloudy water. It's exhausting just to look at it, as I shift from foot to foot. Maybe I stand there for a long time, because a number of people pour around me and into the bar's front door, and some out. I get the sense that I'm in the way, strangely in the way, but still I go on with that smile, now a little more exhausted, just standing there. I wonder what people think of the way I'm standing there.

Rebecca would hate this, always hated to be caught out in the open, doing something odd or embarrassing. She never wanted to be pinned down, singled out, held still, and I always did. Or maybe it was the opposite. But right now she'd be furious if we were together, her arms folded tight, one foot wanting to tap but not wanting to draw any more attention to her.

"People just think I'm waiting for a cab, probably," I'd say to her. Or maybe I actually say it, because just now a couple people shoot looks at me. Rebecca would be furious.

I check my watch, and it's somehow late. I can't tell, however, if it's because I read my watch wrong inside (or just now, but I check it again and get the same number), or whether it actually read similar times inside and out but now that same time just feels later. But it stuns me. How much has my sense of time been warped or shattered? Because whatever I might have thought, it's late. I've already been here a long time. How slow was my ravenous eating, after all? I can picture me from the outside, a ferocious look on my face as I tear into the food, yet slowly, incredibly slowly. The attitude of looting but so off pace.

I need to go.

I remember the night I came home after hanging out late with a semi-friend at McMeniman's down on Germantown, and was barely in the door before there were four arms around me.

Or so it felt—it turned out to be two, both Rebecca's, holding me as though trying to make sure nothing could fly free from me. Then she thrust me back, from fear to anger. *Where—where have you—I've been—what?* Her brown eyes were like a forest fire. *I was out with Brian,* I said. *Remember?* She didn't remember. And then her embarrassment, which wasn't separate from anger, and she breathed hard, casting around as though looking for backup. *I'm sorry,* I said. *Be mad. I know it's because you love me.* And she stopped casting around, and reached both hands up to my cheeks, awash with tenderness. *Always be here,* she said. *Always be here.*

I'm gripping a parking meter, a strangle hold. People shoot glances at me, but this is what brings me back from my panic. There's nothing to second-guess, I tell myself, because there's no decision. There's no whether-or-not-to-leave our apartment. There's only the fact of being already gone.

Rebecca herself taught me some of this, or most of this, determination. The way she fought to bring her organization more funding; the way she'd just keep driving whenever we got lost, refusing to even believe in being lost, damn sure not responding to it; the way she stuck to a regimen of running all the time, even through shinsplints and sore knees. I remember when she got me into the NBA playoffs after my birthday last year, Sixers-Pacers, just by relentlessly pursuing all the favors people owed her until somebody coughed up seats in the twentieth row. That was the game where Matt Geiger and Reggie Miller fought, and everyone in the crowd was chanting *Geiger, Geiger,* both of us, too, and we believed Philly could come back to win from being down 3-0 in the series. Of course, the Sixers went on to lose in six games, but I didn't care—that day, I was just watching Rebecca believe.

But while I've picked up some of her tenacity, I still don't have her sense of direction. I know I'm gone, but not where.

So my feet just start moving, which feels good, and I'm off down Market Street, with the hopping clubs and martini bars, blurry sophisticated neon on both sides. This street, which I guess was once the pits, is rebirthing. People come here on purpose now, struggle for parking just to get into one of the loud, dressy venues. I'm skipping all that, winding drunkenly up the ramp to the bridge leading to Penn's Landing.

The only reason this bridge is needed, I think with resentment, is that this city was built wrong in the first place. It's as though the planners had no interest in the Delaware River, aside from mercantile use and as backdrop for I-95. It wasn't developed for people. I never said anything like this to Rebecca—we had to avoid comparing New York to Philly, because it drove her crazy. She was loyal, anchored, and she could have talked for hours about what made her hometown the best: more colleges and universities than any other U.S. metropolitan area; one-time nation's capital; first zoo; birthplace of ice cream and Reconstructionist Judaism; and all the things that Ben Franklin invented. So strange now to be left holding all the things she held so tight herself.

Nowadays, with the bridges accessing the river, couples wander beside it, stopping to neck at benches or against dirty walls, as long as the weather's nice. There are a few of them scattered around now, mostly gawky and young. One waifish girl wearing lots of makeup—I can even see it in the dark—seems afraid to be out here with a boy she doesn't even know completely, doesn't even know how to know. Could one of them be Rebecca, and the other me? I turn away before I make her afraid myself.

I climb the rest of the way down the edge of the concrete,

where it lips up to keep people out of the Delaware. At night it's beautiful, lit by occasional lamps on our side, and the industrial buildings and aquarium in Camden, on the other side, all of this through the warp and weave of alcohol in my eyes. The beauty is awkward, with me walking along inebriated among the romantic pairs. They are on all sides. I want to cut them out of my peripheral vision. Spotting an empty bench set into a concrete nook overlooking the water, I slump in, my hands in my pockets against the cold. I feel a little sleepy, wonder where I'm going to stay tonight. I had a bed-and-breakfast in mind, I think, but it's probably too late for that. With an upset stomach, I feel like just sitting a minute.

After a second, I feel it—independent from my brain, my face is running, streaming, everything still as all the liquid in my body tries to escape me. Then I'm savage, roughing the tears from my face with my sleeves, and I have to push the sadness away, almost physically, like I'm pushing it with my hands.

The water slaps the side of the concrete. Slaps it. This is a dangerous place—even if I can keep one thought away, others lap up against my mind, carried on the water. And the alcohol is definitely starting to become not good. Now, along with making my stomach sour, it's making the memories sharp before winging them at me. The light press of her palm on my forehead to soothe me while we were in bed, the small, tight sulk of her mouth when she was upset, the time she told me I was the only sane person she knew. Everything honed to where it can be painful. I let the tears come, and then rough them off my face again.

Eventually, I find myself too tired for any more of this. It's as though my body has simply decided *enough*. I'm still drunk, but now neither safe nor unsafe—just too drowsy for anything new to happen inside or outside of me. I know I'm going to fall asleep right here, on this scummy bench, where it's going to get too cold, but since it's a fact, I give in. Oh, the bench is hard.

Rebecca and I had a ritual. We tried to do this every night, at least early on after I moved in and during the wedding planning, and we were only ever thrown off by exhaustion, or fighting, or worse. We did it as we stared hopefully and childishly up at the ceiling, her thick hair all over her pillow and mine, me feeling my short hair crushing into a cowlick. It was her idea, stringing blessings to the end of the day, even though neither of us believed in a kind of active, concrete God who could listen to such things, and really the word *God* was sort of a shorthand for our interest in, or gratitude for, the universe itself. But we would say just a few blessings each, one of us starting *Baruch atah adonai*, Blessed are you, God, the other one finishing it with something:

who gives us enough rest to start again . . .

who helped me find my checkbook today . . .

who brought that gorgeous sunset to Kelly Drive while we ate our sandwiches . . .

who gave me you . . .

who gave me you . . .

Each of us could tell, after some months into this, when the other still had a blessing or two left, and so we'd keep offering *Baruch atah adonai* until the other was definitely done. And then we'd feel our shoulders touching, and one of us would roll toward the other.

It's not a dream, but it's mixed up in one. I feel myself tumbling down the stairs, bruising myself on step after step, jarring my bones against the wood, but it's not a dream, or not quite. I'm half-asleep, stretched out on the scummy bench, still drunk, it could be any time of night, it could be endless night, and I'm being jarred. A tightness in my raging stomach.

"Bum!" a demon spits, looming over me. There are two of them, but it seems like a horde, all around me in that tiny nook, cursing me and making my head flash—bright—with shock, yelling things at me. It's too dark outside, too bright inside, to see anything but their shapes, their jacketed young bodies—they are kids—lashing at me. I feel their spit, or my blood, on my face.

Then it stops. All I do is raise my arms, but I guess the kids wanted at me only as long as I was asleep, and so they leap off onto the main dock and tear away into the night. I hold my arms up, stunned, feeling the aftershocks of pain surfacing in spots on my body, pulsing. Then I lean over the side of the bench. I retch, and then roll back again, sit up. Swooning, I touch the slight wet on my face, taste it. It isn't blood—could be spit, puke, but they never touched my face. Did they touch me at all? When I run my hands over my body, very much still drunk and in shock both, I can't tell. Maybe when it all catches up to me, it will hurt more. Now, though, the aftershocks are in just a few places, and diminishing.

I've been attacked. I lean back on my side, spit the sour out of my mouth. People I couldn't see, two boys waiting to find someone asleep. Nothing like this has ever happened to me before. I am really, I decide, truly in the wilderness. I still hear the water beating against the dock.

Anything can happen to me out here.

I'll Be Home

INCLUDING ME, I know three Jews who go home to their parents to celebrate Christmas. We're sort of a support group for each other, even though our situations are different. Karen's parents, for example, do Christmas just because they're go-along-to-get-along people, and they live in rural Ohio, where it's hard to be a Jew, for sure. Josh's parents, on the other hand, found Christ on a vacation in Canada. I don't know if they're Jews for Jesus or Christians or what, but it makes Josh turn colors, he gets so angry. Me, I'm the oddball of the group, because I converted to Judaism three years ago.

Over those years, my family and I have developed a very polite system to make the season work. Ours is something of a compromise—they can live with me being Jewish, as long as I visit them in Florida to do Christmas with a certain amount of enthusiasm.

This Christmas, my father picks a winding route between the Miami airport and their house in Coral Gables. We don't talk much, but only because driving requires so much of his attention now. He intends the cruise along Miracle Mile to replace conversation, driving me past all the fake-ivy-bedecked shops and the young women in small black dresses and Santa hats. He just hunches over the wheel in his short-sleeved, button-down shirt and occasionally points out especially garish storefronts, which are everywhere in this part of Florida. Whenever I get back from one of these trips and take a taxi into downtown Philadelphia, everything seems wonderfully gray. They tell me they could never live in that part of the country again—it depresses them. Yet they raised me there, once.

When we finally get to my parents' neighborhood, my father relaxes a little—he knows these streets well. "Driving isn't what it used to be," he says apologetically. "Sometimes I think they make the roads narrower and put the stoplights farther away every night while I'm asleep." The houses are all brightly lit— palm trees wrapped in colored bulbs the size of limes, strings of lights along eaves and doorways, glowing plastic nativity scenes on the lawn and/or glowing plastic menorahs in windows. As usual, my parents' is no exception to the general tone. The bulbs wink at me as the car rounds into the driveway.

Hardly anybody can understand why I converted, Jews included. Even my girlfriend Leah calls me a masochist, though she's glad I was already Jewish when she found me. She used to have a tendency to fall for Protestants, which drove her parents crazy. For all kinds of reasons, we've found it really easy to fall in love. Sometimes we just sit around and marvel about it.

Karen, Josh, and I all have significant others. They're as much a part of the support group as we are, because they're so desperately needed. Every one of them Jewish, they hold our hands after we call home and listen to us sigh.

Christmas Eve is tree-decorating and pizza night at my parents' house. Once my mother has gotten my coat off and put a mug of hot cider into my hand, she holds my cheeks and just beams at me. Her face is deep with the lines you get from smiling and laughing all your life, and her green eyes twinkle like crazy. My father then takes me by the arm, leads me to the bare tree. He's developed a ritual about this.

"What do you think?" he asks.

It's a big tree—dense, fat and tall, and it radiates a woodsy darkness out of the corner of the living room. The pair of arm-chairs has been moved away. "It's a beaut," I tell him. It certainly is better than the plastic tree Karen's family supposedly has.

"Well, how about this?" He taps a switch on the wall, and track lighting hits the tree, yanking it out of the shadows. "Boom!" he says. "Jumps right out at you, doesn't it?" I agree that it does.

Going through the boxes of ornaments has become an odd thing for me. Seeing all the rarities from that part of my child-hood makes me feel strangely nostalgic and distant at the same time. It also makes me think about my completely undecorated apartment. It's still very strange to be so willfully ignorant of the Christmas season.

Mom gets Handel's *Messiah* going pretty much right away. The room fills up with the chorus and the orchestra, and the scent of cider, which would be too hot for Florida except that my parents keep the air conditioner on maximum. It helps them to get into the spirit.

My father insists on keeping the track lighting off while we decorate the tree. Colored bulbs, drummer boys, reindeer, stars, glass balls, glass icicles, and Santas wind their way up the branches, each of us stepping back to make sure no spots go undecorated. When every place the eyes might settle holds an ornament, we call it done. The pizza—pineapple—has arrived by then. My father has my mother and me sit down in the armchairs, and hits the switch for the track lighting.

"Boom," I say, popping a cube of pineapple into my mouth.

"It jumps right out at you," Mom finishes.

I don't like sleeping away from my girlfriend. Settling into the oversoft bed, I find myself spooning with what would be Leah's back, my right arm wrapped close around my chest, my left hand cupping under her thigh. I curve around the comforter as though it's her, and get not a bit closer to sleep.

I couldn't call her tonight because she was going to be at a Temple Owls basketball game, having gotten the seats free from Josh and his girlfriend, who have season tickets. Then, Leah said, she would get up early to go out again. She loves Christmas Eve and Day because the whole world is available to her, with Christians too busy to use any of it. She hops between movie theaters and restaurants and whatever museums are open. I wish I could be with her, enjoying the mostly-emptiness of those places, the knowing looks passed between the Muslims and Jews and all the other deviants. But she will be home tomorrow, just to catch my call.

I open my eyes to glance around the room. The light through the window from the other houses' decorations is almost enough to see by. I have never lived here, but my parents have preserved the essence of my high-school era room in here—other guests stay down the hall. I take in the dark shapes of my old things—the shelves full of the first books I ever read, the lumps of stuffed animals in the corner, ice skates laced together and hanging over the closet doorknob. In the half-light, I can almost put aside how old I am, and that the size and shape of the room is somewhat wrong. The comforter, battling the air-conditioned chill, makes me feel secure in the way that children sometimes do. As I wander around the fringes of sleep, I lose some certainty about where and who I am.

It's pretty deep into Christmas morning when I wake up. I can sense the tree and the presents in the living room, and I can almost feel Josh and Karen waking up to the same sensation. I wish we were in touch via walkie-talkies or something. Josh dreads this morning especially. He's Orthodox, though he was raised Conservative and didn't start shifting over until he was at Brandeis. It's almost as though his parents rebelled against *him* after that, after he sent them separate dishes for *milchig* and *fleishig*, started asking them about going to synagogue, testing their Hebrew. Now he and his parents have their territory staked out. They've both got a sort of basic God, but Torah and Jesus face off every time they're all in the same room. My parents and I don't have our territory clearly defined like that, especially since my folks aren't clear on what they believe, except that there should be family traditions.

I lever myself out of bed and head to the bathroom—just to wash my face; we stay in pajamas, in my family, for Christmas morning. It's still sort of strange that there are no stairs to descend on the way to the living room—everything in Florida seems to be one story. But the whole floor is familiarly full of the scent of coffee, and soon the smell of cinnamon french toast will join in. I find both my parents in their armchairs, watching the brightly lit tree and sitting with their hands on their laps like kids who can barely restrain themselves from tearing into the gifts. I pull from my bag the ones I brought, and they're beautifully wrapped —before I converted, they used to be sealed up in brown grocery bags, but now I feel like I have to do better. I lay them in the spots each of my parents has long claimed under the tree.

"Well," my mother says after greeting me and offering me hot and cold beverages, "should we start with stockings?" She is wearing a forest green nightgown, perfectly complementing my father's bright red pajamas. Everybody is smiling fit to burst.

The stocking part is not unlike Hanukkah, actually. Each of the eight days Leah and I exchanged the kinds of things that would fit in stockings—candles, earrings, good chocolate, canisters of film. Here I get very similar gifts, along with batteries, which means that I'm getting something that needs them.

"Don't pay any attention to those batteries," Dad says with an anxious smile.

My father has always been ambivalent about the order of the stockings versus presents, because this way you get clues. But my mother thinks it would be anticlimactic the other way, opening pencils and wind-up toys last.

"What? These are for my old travel alarm clock, right?" I say. We all laugh, relieved.

At the bottom of my stocking is a note I wrote in crazy big print when I was about six years old. It says "Merry Christmas,

Brian! Open this every year and then put it back." I fold it up and return it to the toe, a little sad.

The phone catches us by surprise, right in between the stockings and the big gifts. My mother looks at both of us, almost bewildered, and answers it as though she's not sure what to do. "Hello?" she says. "Oh. Oh, hello. Well, how are you, this . . . this holiday season? Good, goo—oh, you are? Oh! Well, hold on, dear. Why don't I get Brian for you?" She hands it to me with wide eyes, and I take it.

"Hey!" Leah yells. "Guess where I am?"

"Where?" I'm thrilled and scared at the same time.

"Ha! Don't give me that, buster—you've already figured it out," she says. I look around at my parents, who are talking in whispers.

She's at the Miami airport, of course.

Nobody's on the roads as I drive to pick up Leah. The non-Christmas people may be out somewhere, monopolizing places, but they're not here. Maybe they're sleeping in, though it's getting late. My mother has decided to start the french toast while I'm out, because we're falling behind a little. They have both expressed great joy at Leah's arrival, but I don't believe it. It's not that they don't like her—they go on about her each time they visit me—but this is Christmas. Her presence is something like Judaism breaking the rules, sending too many players onto the field.

Me, I feel like I'm leaving my family to go get my family. I drive even faster than the few other cars that are out, in a part of the country where everybody speeds. Josh would tell me to watch myself, because the cops are probably on the watch for speeding Jews on a day like this one, but nothing happens.

You can't go all the way to the gates at this airport, so I meet Leah by the baggage carousels. She is heavily overdressed, in long sleeves, jeans, and a jacket. Naturally, it's cold back in Philly. For a minute, all the carousels seem to stop while we hug. Her black curls smell like her conditioner, which I have come to associate with happiness. Then we step back and hold one another at arm's length—absorbing distance.

"Temple won," she says, smiling sharply, "though they had to scare me by being behind most of the time."

"Bastards," I say.

I walk Leah in ahead of me, like I'm presenting her to my parents. She gets my Mom's arms immediately, and then my Dad's.

"Merry Christmas," she says with a bright smile.

"And happy holidays to you," my mother says. "Are you hungry?" I can smell hot butter and cinnamon.

Leah checks me with a glance and then nods eagerly. "On the plane I had to give my ham and cheese muffin away. Whatever happened to cereal?"

Unlike Josh, Karen tells me there's no conflict at all in her house. Her family is like the Roman Empire, absorbing every tradition that walks by. Some Christmases they have a crèche, wreaths, albums of carols playing. Others they just have the gifts. When Karen gets back from seeing her parents, she is invariably more bossy than when she left. It's the lack of structure at home, she says. Somebody needs to take charge.

Mom's french toast, as always, is so good that it's hard to imagine ever eating any other kind. For a few moments, Leah and I just eat, wrapped up in the pleasure of it. Plus I'm having trouble making conversation, because I can't seem to handle both Leah and Christmas in my head simultaneously. It's like being two people at once—part of me wants to find out what among my gifts needs AA batteries, and part of me wants to huddle with my girlfriend in the air conditioning.

"Wow—this is delicious," Leah says, and my mother thanks her. "Just amazing. Hey, thanks for welcoming me. So here I drop in, right in the middle of everything, huh?"

"No, no," my father says, shaking his fork. "No, no."

"Well, I hope I'm not too much trouble. But so tell me—how do you usually do things around here, anyway? I want to get the full experience."

I want to hug Leah—she's hit on just the right thing to say. But then my mother speaks up.

"We don't really have anything planned," she says, glancing at Dad. "We thought we'd just play it by ear."

I stop chewing and stare at my parents like they are aliens. "Well, weren't we going to open the gifts next?"

"That sounds like fun," Leah says, all bright eyes.

"Oh, that can wait," Mom says. "Wouldn't it be fun to go out?"

I check my watch as though it can explain what's going on.

Dad, Leah, and I spend the rest of the afternoon on a driving tour of Coral Gables and Miami again. Mom's at home, cooking. The roads are still empty, downtown, in the suburbs, everywhere. When we pass Miami Beach, though, Leah asks if we can stop.

When she gets back to Philly, she wants to be able to tell people that she put her feet in the ocean. Dad waits in the car.

"Want to swim for Philadelphia?" I say as we kick our way through the hot sand.

"No bathing suit," she says. The sky is a kind of tropical blue and very few people are out, though I see one family that looks Middle Eastern sprawled out on beach blankets.

"Well, I guess we'll have to stay here, then."

She puts her arms around my chest, sideways, and squeezes me. "Am I messing things up? Should I have stayed home?"

I squeeze her back. "No," I say, though I am really only answering the second question.

Leah keeps her shoes off in the car so the ocean can air dry off her feet. She's amazed at how warm the water was. Her Massachusetts family vacations in Maine, where in August the water will turn you cobalt blue. She showers Miami with compliments, filling the conversational space my father can't while he's driving.

"It takes us fifteen minutes just to get ready to go outside these days," she says, "all the coats and the scarves and the wool socks. Luckily we hardly heat the apartment, so the shock isn't as bad leaving it. You must love it here. Warm all the time!"

My father smiles shyly at her.

Mom greets us at the door in a yellow apron, smiling with pride. "I called the Liebners," she tells Dad, "just to make double sure the dinner I made is kosher. And they say it is. After all, now there's two."

"Critical mass," I say.

We pass by the living room where the tree stands kind of stiffly, as though wondering why it's still surrounded by gifts. The table, again, is set up in the kitchen, though we usually eat this meal in the living room. In fact, the spread is different than usual, too—instead of green beans and mashed potatoes there's wild rice and steamed broccoli. And there's no turkey. It must still be in the freezer; Mom's got a roast cooling on the range. She catches me looking at her.

"Something new, I thought," she says.

I wonder how much time Mom spent running around after all this food, or if she already had it in reserve. She's completely unreadable tonight. Even with all the heat from the oven, she has yet to break a sweat.

After dinner, Leah runs to her bag to get my parents the gift she bought them in Philly. It's wrapped neatly and elegantly in brown paper, which I see she cut from a grocery bag.

"Well, thank you, dear," my mother says, "though we . . . we didn't get you anything, because you don't . . ."

"Oh, no, it's not a Christmas gift in particular. It's just, well, here I show up on your doorstep, so it's more like a thank-you gift."

"Oh, okay then," my mother says, and she begins to open it as though relieved. It's a box full of different teas and gourmet coffees and cocoas. My parents seem to like it.

"So, are you guys going to open your gifts now?" Leah asks.

My parents exchange a glance. "Why don't we play cards instead?"

"You want to save them until later?" I ask.

"Well, who says we have to open them tonight?" my Mom says.

"Who says we have to *open them tonight?*" I repeat. If Karen were here, she would take charge, but she is not.

"Son," my Dad says reasonably, "what's wrong with playing cards for a change?" My mother gives me a smile.

On some level I'm starting to understand. It's not Christmas right now, for them. They can't even go through the motions.

I help my Dad remember the rules to Rummy 500.

That night, I really do spoon with Leah, and she falls asleep easily, exhausted in part from being the big winner in cards. While I listen to her breathe, the front of me becomes completely warm, just on the edge of sweat. Yet the air conditioning remains a force, roaming over my back with cold feet.

Eventually I get up, unspooning myself carefully so as to leave Leah in the same comfortable curve. I tuck blankets all around her to shield her from the chill, and then pad out of the room. Everything is quiet. Usually when I get up to use the bathroom, I can hear my Dad snoring in their bedroom, but now, as I stand still outside my room, everything is perfectly quiet. For a moment, I just absorb it. Then I head for the living room, running my hand along the wall to keep me on track through the dark.

My eyes have started to adjust by the time I get to the living room, partially because neighbors' colored lights shine through the window. I can see the lumpen shape of the Christmas tree spanning the distance from floor to ceiling, and the mounds underneath it. I wonder if we will ever unwrap these things. If we will have to wait until next year. Then I look further around.

They are in the armchairs, my parents, and I see the whites of their eyes, so they are awake. Like me, they're in the dark, staring at the tree, and silent. They sit almost like they did that morning, hands in laps, but without that barely restrained energy. Now they look tired, unsure. Without looking directly into their faces, I sit between the chairs. We sit like this for a long time. I don't know what they are thinking—whether Dad will soon get up to turn on the track lighting, or Mom to make cider, but I am waiting for them to do something. I am waiting for someone to shift at all.

Acknowledgments

Grateful acknowledgment is made to the following journals in which these stories previously appeared, sometimes in different forms:

Aethlon ("Pointing Up"); *Beloit Fiction Journal* ("Fighting," under the title "When Everything Will Ache the Same," and "Nothing Ever Happens in White America"); *Black Dirt* ("Getting Back onto Solid Foods"); *Connecticut Review* ("Rebbetzin"); *Crazyhorse* ("I'll Be Home"); *Crescent Review* ("Misdirections"); *Drexel Online Journal* ("Orange"); *Green Mountains Review* ("Bridesmaid"); *Stickman Review* ("Between Camelots").

This book would not exist without the incredible support of many people. Thanks to Stewart O'Nan for selecting my manuscript for the Drue Heinz Literature Prize, and to Cynthia Miller, Lowell Britson, Maria Sticco, Ann Walston, Deborah Meade, Amy Sykes, and everyone else at University of Pittsburgh Press for making it into a book. I am deeply grateful to the many readers who gave feedback, help, and inspiration on various drafts of these stories, including Carol Church, Heather Lee Schroeder, Tenaya Darlington, Heather Skyler, Dean Bakopoulos, Harry Groome, Jacqueline Lalley, Sarah Van Arsdale, and David Guinn. I also thank my wonderful teachers: Jesse Lee Kercheval, Ellen Lesser, Christopher Noel, Mary Grimm, Douglas Glover, Colleen Moore, and Carol Nehez. Finally, I am profoundly grateful for the longstanding support of my family and, above all, my wife—my great love—Rachel.